A LOVER TOO MANY

When Peter Marlin discovers his wife strangled in their sitting-room suspicion falls heavily on him. After all, she had only recently returned home after an unexplained absence of several months; and during that time Peter had taken up with someone else. After the inquest Inspector Crow of Scotland Yard arrives to make further inquiries.

A LOVER TOO MANY

A LOVER TOO MANY

by

Roy Lewis

Dales Large Print Books
Long Preston, North Yorkshire,
BD23 4ND, England.

British Library Cataloguing in Publication Data.

Lewis, Roy
    A lover too many.

    A catalogue record of this book is
    available from the British Library

    ISBN   978-1-84262-603-0 pbk

First published in Great Britain 1969 by William Collins

Published in Large Print 2008 by arrangement with
Mr Roy Lewis

Dales Large Print is an imprint of Library Magna Books Ltd.

Printed and bound in Great Britain by
T.J. (International) Ltd., Cornwall, PL28 8RW

CHAPTER 1

1

He came out, blinking, into the sunshine. Nothing seemed to have changed. There was the usual roar of traffic from the High Street, funnelling down through the narrow lane. Sunlight lanced black shadows against the walls, slicing the lane in two, black and grey. People were still walking, talking in the High Street. Nothing seemed to have changed.

Except Peter Marlin.

The others had gone. He had been the last to leave. Shirley had gone; she hadn't glanced at him. It was not surprising; he had been conscious of the way people in the courtroom looked sideways at her and he had no doubt that their eyes reflected the thoughts in their minds. Shirley Walker and Peter Marlin...

And Jeannette.

He moved away from the doors and paced slowly down through the narrow, paved lane towards the High Street. It was an old lane, as old as the town, medieval. It hadn't changed.

But *he* had – he must have. How else could

he have sat there, outwardly unemotional, when the suggestions were made, the innuendoes thrown at him? How was it that he could not bring himself to speak in his defence, in Shirley's defence?

More important, *when* had he changed? To-day? Or months ago, when Jeannette had returned?

The coroner had, of course, overstepped the mark.

'It is not for me to pass comment,' Potter had said heavily, 'on the moral aspects of the circumstances. It is not for me to suggest that the – ah – affair that seems to have developed between Mr Marlin and Miss Walker has any bearing on the death of Mrs Marlin. There is no positive evidence to show that any link exists. We are aware that Mrs Marlin knew of the affair, that she learned of it shortly after her return. It would seem that the whole thing was over and forgotten for her – she and Mr Marlin were living together – ah – reasonably amicably. So the evidence does not seem to suggest that the death of Mrs Marlin would necessarily be important to Mr Marlin's liaison with Miss Walker. Indeed, there is no evidence to suggest that the relationship between Mr Marlin and Miss Walker has any connection whatsoever with the death of Mrs Marlin…'

In which case his words were irrelevant. In which case all the coroner was doing was relaying gossip. But gossip of the worst kind, gossip that merely started people's minds turning over, thinking about what could have happened, mulling over the possible relationships that could have existed between Shirley Walker and Jeannette and Peter Marlin.

Relationship! Between the two women a positive dislike, that was certain. But where did he stand, where had he stood? Weakly, indecisively. That was the way he had always been, as far as Jeanette was concerned.

He turned into High Street and thought briefly of stopping off at the Blue Dragon for a cup of coffee, but then he knew that it was only an excuse for not returning to the office and he cursed and hurried on. He'd have to go in, walk past Betty's wide eyes, bespectacled, curious behind her typewriter, walk past Joan's office, the ante-room to his own. They would say nothing. But they would be aware. And after a decent interval, when he'd had time to sit in his leather chair and gnaw at the time, Joan would bring in some papers for signature, a query from a client, a letter to be answered, a problem to be solved.

The sooner it was over the better. Then perhaps things could go back to normal. As if normalcy was what he had ever wanted.

'Peter!'

Marlin stopped, and turned his head. Threading away from a small knot of people across the other side of the road was the tall, slim figure of John Sainsby. His arm was raised.

Peter waited dully. John was grey suited, dark waistcoated as usual. He had the formula white collar, striped shirt. He moved gracefully, as always, his careful, predatory face pale, his moustache neat and precise and formal. As he trotted to the pavement, his black briefcase clutched in his right hand, he was smiling nervously. Peter moved away, and John Sainsby fell into step beside him. It irritated Peter; John Sainsby always walked in step.

'It's over.'

Peter nodded. All over.

'The … er … the verdict?'

'Murder,' said Peter harshly, 'by person or persons unknown.'

Sainsby was quiet for a moment, his mouth puckered under the neat moustache. His shoes echoed Peter's, rhythmically.

'There's little I can say,' he murmured. 'Little that anyone can say, now.'

'That's right,' grunted Peter.

Sainsby twitched his cuff free from entanglement with the handle of his briefcase.

'You had Potter as coroner … did everything go all right?'

Peter quickened his pace in anger.

'You know Potter as well as I, John. You can imagine the hares he flushed, the irrelevancies he floundered out into open inquest ... a really *open* inquest.'

'One of these days,' Sainsby said thoughtfully, 'someone will be suing him for slander.'

'In a coroner's inquest? For statements made in the course of his duty? You know your law better than that, John!'

Sainsby's legs were longer than Peter's, but they still marched in unison with his. Sainsby was looking down at them.

'Did he say anything ... particularly damaging?'

'If you mean did he drag Shirley Walker into the whole thing,' Peter said bitterly, 'the answer is yes. If you mean did he hint at the fact that we'd been lovers–'

'Peter, really, I–'

'–the answer is, again, yes. If you mean will people now be thinking that perhaps I, or Shirley, know more about the whole thing than we pretend I'm damn' sure, again, that the answer will be yes! The blasted man ought to be compulsorily retired!'

'He hasn't long to go,' soothed Sainsby, his face a little pink.

'For me,' grunted Peter, 'and for Shirley Walker, it's irrelevant, the damage is done.'

He turned into Green Street and ran up the steps of Abbey House ahead of John.

2

The sign on the glass doors before him proclaimed in faded gold lettering *Martin, Sainsby and Sons, Solicitors and Notaries Public, Commissioners for Oaths.*

The stone face of Abbey House was grimed with age. The offices of Martin, Sainsby and Sons were situated on the first floor: they had always been there, since Abbey House was built in the eighteen-thirties. The world around Abbey House, and inside it, had changed over the years, but Martin, Sainsby and Sons remained. Martin had died in 1880, leaving no heirs, and Sainsby and his two sons had soldiered on. The first son had died a bachelor; when the second son died, in 1930, he had left one male heir to carry on. Stephen Sainsby was that son and he was still there, upstairs, assisted now and being dragged, complaining, into the modern business world, by his nephew John Sainsby and Peter Marlin.

It was perhaps Stephen Sainsby's impatience with modern business methods and with the changing nature of the pressures of his profession that had caused him to look to other fields of late. He and his family had had a long Liberal tradition, locally; his father had spent a few years away from the business in political campaigning and had succeeded in winning a seat in the

Commons for a brief period, before returning to the quiet office when it became apparent that in the Commons his influence upon policy was going to be minimal and he was in any case unlikely to regain the seat he lost in the general election.

But his father's disappointment had not soured Stephen Sainsby's ambitions in that direction. They had lain dormant for most of his life, but now that the firm was showing rising profit margins, and he felt the tug of impatience at its progress (since it was due to no effort on his part) he had begun to fly political kites more positively. And it was rumoured that preferment was perhaps not too distant.

Peter mounted the stairs to the first floor and pushed open the glass-panelled door. As he'd guessed, Betty was sitting there, plump and solid as a fat hen, with her myopic eyes gazing at him from behind her horn-rimmed spectacles. He said nothing to her, raising a hand in brief greeting before turning through the door to the corridor beyond and up the short, four step flight of stairs to the door marked 'Peter Marlin, LL.B., Solicitor of the Supreme Court.'

He grimaced mentally as he always grimaced at the sight of the plaque: Stephen thought it good for business that their 'credentials' should be displayed. Peter thought it pompous and unnecessary, but Stephen was the senior partner.

In the ante-room, sitting neatly behind her desk, was Joan Shaw. She raised her red head as he came in and smiled. She had good teeth, a good figure, and was remarkably efficient. She had everything a man could need in a secretary. He knew it and, he suspected, so did she. And like the good secretary she was she said nothing now, as he passed through the red-carpeted room to his own office. There was just the brief smile; no questions, no curiosity. None that showed, anyway.

Peter closed his door behind him. It was strange how much safer he felt, shut in this room. Safer, and calmer. Perhaps it was because of the hours he had spent here alone: the hours he had spent hard at work in the early years with the firm until he became a partner, the longer hours, midnight hours, that he had spent here during the months after Jeannette left him. The room had become so familiar to him: the smell of the leather arm-chair, the softness of the green carpet, the pale warmth of the magnolia painted walls, the hard dark wood of the desk, broad, comfortable, executive. Peter grunted to himself. Executive! He'd never before admitted to himself that buying this desk had been an action dictated by a need to feel that he was really in the executive class.

Maybe that was what a working-class

background did for you. For Jeannette it had meant other things.

But now Jeannette was dead. The coroner had said so firmly, and had said other things besides.

Real business executives kept bottles of whisky in a drawer or in a gleaming decanter, cut glass, on a shelf. In Peter's drawers there were papers, a dictaphone, clips, a paper punch, rubbish; on his shelves there were books, *Curtis and Ruoff on Registered Conveyancing, Hill and Redman's Law of Landlord and Tenant, Accounting Requirements of the Companies Acts, Stone's Justices Manual.* They marched shoulder to red, black, green, blue and grey shoulder, drugs that had dulled his sensibilities when Jeannette had left him, far better than whisky could ever have done. They had befriended him then, in the dark days, they had filled his mind and they had made him a better lawyer; the room had warmed him and held him, and it comforted him now. It was *his,* a place to flee to then, and perhaps again now.

The leather sighed as he dropped into the arm-chair. The sky was cloudy. There was an old bird's nest against the drainpipe outside the window. It had been built there when Jeannette was alive. Now it was old and abandoned.

The intercom buzzed.

Peter flicked the switch and Joan's voice,

harshened, impersonalised, gritty, intruded into the silent room.

'Mr Marlin, I have a request from Mr Gaines that you telephone him this afternoon. Would you like to make the call now?'

This way lay quick forgetfulness.

'Yes, please, Joan. Get him for me straight away – and I suppose you have other matters for my attention?'

'I'll bring them in as soon as you've finished your call to Mr Gaines.'

'Thank you.'

The intercom went dead.

Just three minutes later the telephone rang and Peter closed the file he had been staring at dully, to lift the receiver.

'Peter?'

'Hallo, Sam. I gather you wanted to have a word with me.'

'Yes, I rang earlier this morning. I'm sorry, I'd forgotten that you'd be at the coroner's inquest–'

If he really had, thought Peter, he'd have been the only one in town who had suffered such a lapse of memory.

'–how did things go?'

'As well as could be expected,' replied Peter dryly.

There was a short silence.

'I'm sorry, Peter, that was a stupid question... I imagine the verdict was murder by persons unknown.'

'It was.'

'Yes ... anyway, we don't want to talk about that. It's over, finished. I just wanted to have a word with you about the meeting to-morrow. Can you pick me up at Grey-gables? The old lady'll do her nut, but I'm afraid that I had a slight contretemps with a lamp-post last night.'

'Serious?'

'Well, it may add a scar or two, but not where my manly beauty will be affected. The Jag is somewhat bent, however. I can count on a lift, then?'

'Of course.'

'Er ... Peter, look, this meeting to-morrow – you know I'm no great shakes at this legal stuff, and I'm just along for the ride at the meeting, as a representative, of the trust holdings, but what exactly is going on? I don't quite get the picture from the agenda.'

Peter hesitated.

'It's ... er ... it's a long story, Sam...'

'Try me, shortly, in short syllables.'

'Well, basically, I suppose, it's nothing more than an attempt at a takeover of the companies in which your trust holdings are placed by Amalgamated Industries, Ltd. Just that.'

'And you *support* the takeover, Peter?'

Again Peter hesitated.

'In principle ... yes, I do. As solicitor to the trust I've looked closely at the deal and I think that it will do a lot of good for the trust holdings.'

'Who's this chap Jackson, Peter?'

Peter went cold.

'Jackson?'

'He's named as the character who'll get a seat in the boards of the trust companies if Amalgamated Industries take over.'

'You seem to have read the notices pretty closely,' remarked Peter in a controlled tone, 'for someone who doesn't know what's going on.'

Sam Gaines laughed. It was on a high pitch that somehow lacked masculinity, a girl's party laugh. But then, Sam went to more than his share of parties.

'I didn't say I hadn't read the papers that came with the agenda – just that I didn't understand them. Do you know this chap Jackson?'

'No. Look, Sam, I'm sorry, but I'm pretty busy at the moment – I think it better that we have a word about it all to-morrow when I pick you up in the car. Mrs Gaines well?'

'Sound as the proverbial ancient bell. Right, Peter me lad, I'll see you to-morrow and you can give me a rundown on the whole swindle then. Okay?'

'I'll see you at Greygables about ten a.m.'

When Peter replaced the telephone his hands were damp. A rundown on the whole swindle. Gaines could have chosen his

18

words with more care.

There was a light tap on the door. It was Joan. She came in with a sheaf of papers in her hand. The letters for signature she placed in front of him. He cast his eyes swiftly over them, more by habit than anything else, for he well knew that he could rely on her, and his eyes took nothing in to his brain on this occasion. He was still preoccupied with Gaines's phrase. And his own feeling of discomfort, the quickness of his pulse.

'And there are these three conveyances, Mr Marlin. They are now due for completion this afternoon. Shall I instruct–'

'Bill,' said Peter firmly. Bill Daly was not the most senior legal executive in the firm, but he was the most capable in conveyancing matters. He should have crossed over into articles years ago, but maybe at thirty-eight now he was too old to start. Stephen Sainsby would certainly think so.

'Anything else, Joan?'

She was looking at him carefully when she said, 'Nothing that can't be dealt with without worrying you, Mr Marlin.'

He stared at her, and a slow smile touched his face. She was a better secretary than he deserved.

'I get the message, Joan. You think I ought to take the day off.'

'After the coroner's inquest–'

'I think,' he interrupted, 'that solid work is a better way of forgetting problems than lying back and worrying about them.'

'I know.'

A silence settled between them. His eyes held hers, and he was aware of their softness. With a slight surge of embarrassment he realised that their sympathy was for him. Even as the awareness came to him, her precision was back.

'You'll be in and available, then, Mr Marlin. Er … just one thing. May I leave a little earlier to-day? You see, I–'

'Be my guest,' smiled Peter. 'Do you know, Joan, you've been working for me for what, five years? And till now you've never asked to leave early. Not once. Explanations aren't necessary. After all, there can't be many more attractive women in town.'

She had half turned away from him, and he suddenly meant the words, more than he'd imagined, as he was aware of the neatness of her figure. Joan Shaw was not tall, nor was she a striking beauty, but her red hair framed an oval face that was well proportioned; her eyes were friendly, her smile warm. Her figure was unflamboyant, but one a male could appreciate. With a positive appreciation.

'Thank you, Mr Marlin.'

For what? He was confused as the door closed behind her. Thanks for the thoughts?

Had they been spoken or had they stayed in his head? What was in his head? He had looked at Joan differently, just now. As a woman? When had he last thought of a woman's body?

Jeannette. Jeannette's body. But it had been without life. It had been there at his feet and the warmth and the life and the loveliness had left it as it lay sprawled unfashionably on the floor. Unfashionably. How Jeannette would have hated that word. How she would have hated the sight of her own lovely face, twisted, a tongue swollen and bitten between bloodied teeth.

She would not have wanted any man, not even Peter, to see her like that.

Desperately, Peter turned to his desk and his papers. But concentration evaded him. The papers lay there, solid and positive in the problems they raised. Matrimonial Homes Act 1967. It would be of assistance in the Davies case. '...*Where one spouse is entitled by virtue of section 2 above to a charge on an estate or interest in a dwelling house and the charge is registered in accordance with subsection (6) or (7) of that section, it shall be a term of any contract...*' The words were incomprehensible, they were cloaked by the dark image of a woman's ungainly shape, sprawled in death on a rumpled carpet.

It was an image that was put to flight only by the insistent intercom.

'Mr Marlin, Mr Stephen would like you to come up to his office as soon as it is convenient.'

It was convenient.

3

'Come in, my boy!'

Stephen Sainsby's office was the largest on the first floor. Its window overlooked the High Street and the muted sound of traffic drifted through the double glazing like the drone of summer bees. The room was wide, the desk was central, the cupboard containing the whisky and the sherry and the gin lurked in mahogany splendour in the far corner and Stephen Sainsby was facing it, his back towards Peter. He was taking out some glasses.

Peter raised his eyebrows to John Sainsby, who stood with one nervous hand on his uncle's desk. John knew as well as Peter that the drinks rarely came out for the partners; the occasional influential client was offered something, the partners only when something important was in the wind.

John Sainsby made no facial reply to Peter's quizzical eyebrows. He looked away.

'Whisky, my boy?'

'I think that would be rather pleasant,' replied Peter carefully and walked towards

22

the desk. Over his shoulder Stephen Sainsby said,

'Take a seat, Peter, take a seat.'

Peter did as he was told.

He observed Stephen Sainsby as the senior partner poured the drinks. The man was fifty-eight now, but presented an upright, handsome figure, and his waist was trim. He went to a good tailor, as the cut of his grey suit showed; his hairdresser charged the highest prices in town, and Stephen's white hair gave him a distinguished appearance, swept back carefully, trimmed neatly at the nape of the neck, the merest hint of sideburns. His lean, ascetic face was profiled to Peter and lined with concentration as he poured the drink, gold in the faceted glass. Stephen Sainsby did everything with concentration and, he had often insisted to Peter and John, it always paid dividends. He was turning now, proffering the glass to Peter, an inch of white shirt-cuff displayed, long, lean, hard fingers holding the glass lightly.

'A dash of soda?'

Peter agreed.

'I'll have the same, Uncle.'

'I thought you would do so.'

John sat down, across from Peter. Stephen Sainsby elegantly perched himself on the edge of his desk, one leg swinging in smartly creased grey flannel.

He raised his glass and his smile showed the slightly age-stained teeth of his lower jaw, contrasting with the bleached dentures above.

'Peter, John – your health,' he said softly – 'and the health of the firm.'

The whisky was warm in Peter's throat. He was suddenly aware that he had needed it, needed it all morning. He took a second sip, more slowly. Stephen Sainsby was not looking at him, but at the glass which he had placed on the desk.

'Do you know I've been in this firm all my life, Peter? That's silly, of course you do. You know its history as well as I. You know how I came in at sixteen, took articles and qualified, saw the others die ... and then there was John, and there was you.'

He paused ruminatively.

'Just forty years... You know, Peter, it's a strange thing. I've seen this firm as a living entity and I've seen it grow from a solid, respected business into an efficient modern one – and I've seen where the credit for that lay.'

Peter could not suppress the glance of surprise in John's direction. John's head was bent, staring into his glass. There they both were, uncle and nephew, gazing in rapt concentration at puddles of whisky in cut glass tumblers.

'It's lain with you two youngsters. You two

boys came into this firm, John as a partner, you as an assistant and then later as a partner, and by dint of your efforts – and I admit here that I was of little assistance to you, but then, old dogs abhor new tricks – you dragged this firm out into the harsh sunlight of modern business techniques...'

It was unlike Stephen Sainsby. Peter wondered vaguely if he was rehearsing political speeches and phraseology, but a warning ticked through his brain.

'...and we saw the results in the rising profit margins, the increased business from commerce in the area, the new respect that appeared in the industrial community. True, the kind of business that we were transacting was changing in its character, the old family firm of former days was disappearing as such, but who could argue against such progress? I watched, and I wondered, and in the end, for all my opposition, and the difficulties I raised, I knew. I knew that you and John, you both had the interests of the firm at heart, you wanted what was best for the firm, you had, in a word, come to look upon the firm as I had always looked upon it. As an entity. As something alive, and worth preserving.'

Stephen raised his glass and took a slow drink. He turned his head, and his eyes were benign as they looked into Peter's. But his mouth was brutal.

'And if you stay with the firm, Peter, you'll kill it!'

Peter's skin was cold. John's head had jerked, as though away from a knife, but he had not looked up. He had known what was coming; it was just the method of presentation that had surprised him.

'What the hell are you talking about, Stephen?'

Peter's tone was calm and even. This surprised him. Nothing surprised Stephen Sainsby.

'It is really quite clear, Peter. The way you – and John – have worked in this firm makes it clear to me that you have a great respect for its traditions. You have regarded it in the same light as I. You may not realise, Peter, that I was fully aware of the time you put into the business, of the long evenings at your desk. You may not realise that–'

'Stop wrapping it up in cotton-wool,' cut in Peter. 'Get to the point.'

Stephen's tone remained smooth.

'The point is quite clear. I know the regard you must have for the firm. I know that you will now see that your continued existence as a partner within the firm can only do it harm, and this, I am sure, you would want to avoid.'

'I don't understand. Why should my presence in the partnership damage the firm?'

'Need I spell it out?' queried Stephen

softly, his eyes narrowing slightly. Peter knew what the reasons would be but wanted to hear them, in the open. Of late, too much had been left unsaid, too much had been hidden and secret.

'Spell it out!'

Stephen shrugged carefully, and stood up to half turn from Peter. His elegant fingers were laced together.

'It can do the firm no good,' he remarked quietly, 'to have as a partner the husband of a woman who was recently murdered by an unknown assailant.'

The silence was expectant, but Peter sat doggedly, waiting. With a sigh of impatience, Stephen continued.

'Particularly when it is common local gossip that the man in question was interrogated by the police concerning his whereabouts at the time of the murder.'

'Uncle–'

Stephen Sainsby raised his hand and John subsided unhappily.

'And even more so when it comes out into the open that the same man had been conducting an illicit affair with a … woman living in this town. You did ask me to spell it out. Those are the reasons. The continued presence of such a man in such a situation can do nothing other than damage to the firm. As far as I am concerned, therefore, my boy, I am faced with the painful task of asking you to withdraw from the firm. The partnership must be dissolved.'

'You can't do it, not just like that.'

'Don't be a fool, Peter. I know you to be a better lawyer than that. Your remark was an emotional, irrational one. Need I quote chapter and verse to you? Our partnership deed is open to dissolution on a number of grounds – not least of which is by one of us giving notice to the others. There is another – where a partner has been guilty of conduct calculated to prejudicially affect the carrying on of the business. Does not the glove fit? Has not your conduct been so prejudicial?'

Peter felt anger rising within him, but he curbed it, dragging his eyes away from Stephen's sneering mouth to John.

'What about you – where do you stand in this?'

John's narrow head jerked up. He did not look at Peter but at Stephen. There was defiance in his eyes.

'I damned well don't agree–'

'In principle,' complemented Stephen smoothly, 'but John was never one to stand by his principles. I had hoped that this could be settled amicably and quietly–'

'If you want me out of the partnership on that ground,' began Peter and then irritatingly finished his drink as the others waited – 'you'll have to do it in court.'

Stephen Sainsby sneered impatiently.

'We can dissolve this partnership by notice–'

'Which will have to run its course,' added Peter quietly.

'You mean you'll hang on to the bitter end,' Stephen snarled.

Peter stood up.

'Why should I hurry to bow out? We have agreements to resolve. There's the question of my share of the partnership. Have you worked out what it's worth, Stephen? And the notice – better check the agreement, Stephen: it must be in writing, and duly served, you know!'

'You're making things blasted difficult, Marlin!' Stephen said, coming forward on stiff legs, angry as a bantam.

Peter's own anger, till now controlled, flashed through.

'Difficult for whom? For *you*, surely! For the firm perhaps, for a little while, though you and I and John all know that this will blow over and be forgotten like any nine days' wonder. But basically and essentially for *you*, Stephen, you and your stupid political ambitions! Has Sir Peter Leonard been breathing down your neck? Has the Lord Lieutenant of the County been on the phone of late? Has Lady Fortescue not invited you to her daughter's coming out? For God's sake don't mouth sanctimonious platitudes about the firm to me, Stephen – tell the truth for once!'

'The truth,' hissed Stephen Sainsby, 'is that written notice dissolving the partnership will be on your desk by five o'clock this afternoon.'

When he had left the room Peter regretted the rude gesture he had then made to the old man: it had brought a contemptuous and supercilious twist to Stephen Sainsby's face. It had made the man feel that he had won.

As, of course, he must do.

And Peter's room was now different. For it was not his room. Maybe it had cocooned him in those days and nights, but it had been the firm's premises all the time. The fact that he had been part of the firm was of no consequence, for the order was changing. Within a month, once the financial details were settled he would be out. Martin, Sainsby and Sons would no longer hold open doors to him.

He needed another drink. Joan looked up at him as he walked quickly out. She opened her mouth to say something but no sound came. Perhaps she half guessed what was wrong, from the sight of his face. If she didn't, she would soon know. Stephen wouldn't type the notice himself.

He had reached the steps to the street when he heard his name called. It was John, hurrying down the stairs behind him.

Stephen Sainsby's nephew stood looking at him unhappily.

'I'm sorry about that, Peter. But … there's not a thing I can do.'

For a moment Peter almost burst out with an angry retort but depression suddenly washed over him.

'No,' he agreed shortly. 'There was nothing you could do.'

It was, after all, the Sainsby family firm.

'Not that it makes much difference, anyway,' mumbled John unhappily, 'not in the long run. The firm will die with Stephen.'

'I don't understand.'

'I'm thinking of leaving too. Stephen doesn't know yet, but I'm thinking of going.'

'Going? Where? Why?'

John shrugged. He turned his lean face to the sunlit street.

'I'm thinking of going to the Bar. It will – it will suit my talents more than–'

'Don't be a bloody fool!'

John shook his head, unhappily.

'You – you don't understand. I – well, I don't know, things aren't going as they should, and–'

John turned suddenly and went back through the glass doors. Peter shouted after him.

'Don't be a bloody fool!'

Betty's eyes would be round with bespectacled disbelief.

Peter drove home carefully.

4

The square-built, green-tiled house stared stonily at him as he swung the car into the drive. The tall bushes that lined the path made no sound to him as he walked past: there was no breeze to rustle through their thick, overgrown branches.

And inside the house it was silent too, soft-carpeted and hushed. There had been a period, after Jeannette had died, when he had thought that peace would never return to the house. There was the coming and going of the police photographers, the fingerprint experts, the constables and the inspectors, two of them. There were the local reporters. There were the morbid sightseers who gawped from the driveway, and the bolder, more inquisitive ghouls who came up to the house to peer in at the windows and gabble at the panes. It had been a wearing time, a difficult time, particularly since his nerves had been frayed by the insistent questioning as to his whereabouts, his relationships with his wife, her address when she had left him, her character (as if he really knew her friends), her enemies, her acquaintances – and his.

It was fortunate that Joan Shaw had been

able to verify the statement that he had made to the police, to the effect that he had been working at the office at the very time that Jeannette had died. And it was a thirty-five minute drive from the office to the house – Jeannette had wanted a house away from the town, in the 'more respectable areas, darling, more in keeping with your *undoubted* status in the community…'

Peter closed the door behind him. The kitchen door faced him and he hesitated. He should have something to eat: his lunch had been non-existent, with the morning inquest unsettling him. But right now he needed a drink.

He turned into the sitting-room, and walked across to the cocktail cabinet. It was a piece of tasteless affectation that Jeannette had chosen for the offence it would give to Peter. There was also the ridiculous little chiming clock, all gilt and cheap, tawdry, imitation. It was of such unimportant stuff that quarrels were made. With a liberal hand Peter poured himself a whisky. It was the best, equal to Stephen Sainsby's. Jeannette would have seen to that. Peter took a stiff gulp from the glass, then sat down with his back to the French windows that overlooked the long narrow lawn at the back of the house, flanked by the enormous rose-bed that Jeannette had planted, then paid a gardener to keep in trim. Last summer the roses had bloomed in magnificence; recent rain had dulled them this year and since Jeannette's death the gardener had not come and the weeds had thickened the soggy base of the rose-trees.

Since Jeannette's death... It was perhaps not strange that he should now measure everything by that event. It was hardly surprising that he should think of her as she was before he saw the trickle of blood from her bitten tongue, think of what she said, what she did, what she was, before he had entered this room and switched on the light and had seen the blue of her dress and the green of the carpet and the darkness of her face, blonde hair swirling crazily across her eyes, one leg twisted under her, a fist clenched in agony—

'The lights were not on?' they had queried. 'The doors, the windows were unforced?'

What the hell did he know about it? What the hell did they expect him to know? He got himself another drink and started back to his chair; half-way there he changed his mind, went back for the bottle, then slumped down to the settee with glass and bottle. Some of the whisky spilled on his jacket as he poured out another drink. He put the bottle on the carpet and tilted the glass to his lips. The sky was cloudy. It had been a clear night when Jeannette had died.

Hell. He had to get her out of his mind.

Peter downed the whisky and poured another, then rose and walked across to the cabinet where Jeannette had kept all her records and tapes. He pulled out one tape and stared at it, oblivious of the tumble of the others. Many of them would be current pops: he had struck lucky first time – Dvorak's 'New World Symphony.' It would do. Jeanette had catholic tastes.

In everything.

Had had.

Did he really mean what his thoughts inferred? Where had she gone – correction, to whom had she gone, if anyone, when she had left him? Did it matter?

Not any more. She was dead, and he was wallowing in Dvorak and whisky and self analysis and self pity. And horror. Don't forget the horror, he thought as the music washed over him and he still saw the blackened tongue and the bloodied teeth. Don't forget the horror.

How had it been in the interval between her death and Potter's bumbling inquest? A strain, certainly, a difficult, horrible time but different from the way things were this afternoon. There had been *people* around and he hadn't been alone. All right they were not real people, not friends, or relations, just police and ghouls and sightseers and reporters, but they were people of a sort. And in his anger at them and frustration at them he hadn't had time to think too much, as he was thinking now – of the sunshine of their courtship, of the excitement of their marriage, of the pain of her going away, of the bite of pride and the dulling millstone of work, of the searing agony of her return...

The day she had come back... He had just returned from Moorside...

Moorside. The whisky was warm inside his throat and the sun was breaking through. The horns soared on the tape and Peter's head fell back drowsily on the cushions of the settee.

He slept.

When he woke he was cold and there was a dark stain on the carpet where the whisky bottle, kicked over some time ago by his dangling foot, had gulped out its contents to the receptive carpet. He swore, not for the stained carpet but for his hammering head. There was another bottle in the cabinet; he rose groggily and walked across to get it. A stiff dose, to chase down the two white headache powders he clumsily pulled out of the medicine cabinet in the bathroom. The bathroom mirror showed him a pale face, paler for the contrast of his dark hair and eyebrows. His mouth looked discontented, even petulant – they were not words which he had previously thought applicable to himself. He bared his teeth: they were sound, and even, at least. With a shrug he took the powders and the whisky. Whisky, water and headache powders. Wasn't it dangerous, liquor and drugs? What wasn't dangerous?

The steps seemed elongated as he walked down the stairs.

Another drink. Stupid. When he had drifted off to sleep something pleasant had warmed him. Now he was depressed again. Music. That's what it was. The tape had ended long ago: there was now only the hum of the playback. The sky – no, it was darkening now. People: it was the thought of people that had warmed him, people and music.

And yet it wasn't – not people, just one person. At Moorside.

Shirley.

He wanted her company, and he wanted the whisky and he wanted music. Unsteadily, with his head still thumping, he walked into the sitting-room, tucking the whisky bottle under his arm. The music tapes lay in an untidy jumble: he grabbed five or six of them and almost dropped the bottle. He put the tapes and the bottle down and walked to the kitchen, pulled an old paper carrier out of the waste-bin, lurched back into the sitting-room and stuffed tapes and bottle into the bag.

It bulged.

He kept one hand under it and one arm around it as he walked out of the front door, pulling the door closed behind him with his foot. The bang echoed in his skull.

With the paper bag dumped on the back seat of the car he reversed carefully into the road, and drove away from the house.

'Now steady as she goes. With the way your reputation lies in shreds at the moment, with dear old Stephen frowning at you and John looking on unhappily, with Potter mouthing stupidities, and Betty thrilling vicariously each time you step through the office, and Joan being her efficient self in spite of it all, it would simply not do if you were now to be taken into custody by the local constabulary on a charge of being drunk in charge of a motor-car and driving to the danger and detriment of the general public–'

Peter realised that he was talking to himself and stopped at once. Aware of his intoxication, he began to drive more slowly: he was not infected with the common alcoholic bravado that he had seen in certain of Jeannette's friends when they had come to her parties at the house. Then, suddenly conscious of the fact that police cars sauntered suspiciously after vehicles that appeared to be moving too slowly, Peter increased the pressure on the pedal and moved into top gear.

He ran the car down through the town. The street lights were on and the neon lit signs flashed cheerily at him. When the crossroads loomed up he stopped carefully, took a good look each way and moved on. The slope of Gladstone Hill took some of the power out of the engine and he slipped into third: he was driving too slowly again, for the car usually sailed up here.

Usually. When had he last driven up Gladstone Hill? It seemed a long time ago. It *was* a long time ago.

When he swung round the bend at the top of the hill the town twinkled at him in the basin below: the moor stretched away darkly to his right. The line of bungalows huddled together just below the skyline: his headlights would be blazoning the hill for watchers down below.

A mile farther on there was the copse, and then the one small bungalow, squat, with leaded windows that reflected his headlights, staring at him in surprise as he turned into the narrow drive. Why shouldn't they? They hadn't seen him in quite a while.

And yet Shirley didn't seem surprised when she saw him leaning there in the doorway, one hand out to press again at the bell, the other still clutching the paper bag to his chest. She simply stood there. The light was behind her and her face was not clear to him but he knew there was no surprise in it. The flatness of her voice told him that.

'Peter.'

Just that.

He was deflated. There had seemed some point in coming out: he had felt a need to be with her, near her, with a drink, and soft music. People. Jeannette.

He could say nothing, and he stood foolishly looking at her standing in the doorway. It was a mistake. He shouldn't have come. He shook his head and half turned away and his foot slipped on the step. He fell to one knee, but kept a tight grip on the bag.

'Peter! Are you all right?'

'Hell!' he commented bitterly, feeling the red gravel bite at his knee.

'You've been drinking.'

When she thus stated the obvious her hand touched his shoulder.

'You'd better come inside.'

And there he was, on the settee, in the small, simply furnished sitting-room that he knew so well, with the paper bag at his feet and Shirley frowning at him.

'You've cut your knee,' she said abruptly, and left him. Peter gazed at the tear in his trouser leg and saw the stain of blood. When Shirley came back with a bowl of hot water and a first aid package he reached for the paper bag. The warmth of the room had revived his spirits.

'You want that I should take a snort before ya operate, Doctor? Seein' you got no anaesthetic?'

He waved the whisky bottle at her. She

didn't smile.

Foolishness, and sobriety, came back as he sat there with one trouser leg rolled up. Shirley bathed the small wound, squeezing out some tiny pieces of gravel. She said nothing until there was a small patch of plaster over the cut. Then she looked up at him.

'Why did you come here, Peter?'

He looked down at the plaster, then carefully rolled down the trouser leg. He'd have to wear the grey suit to the meeting to-morrow.

'I really do feel like a little boy, falling down and cutting my knee.'

'I asked you a question.'

In the time Peter had known her he had never heard her speak sharply, as she did now. He looked at her. Her dark hair was the same as always, cut fairly short, curling naturally at the nape of her neck, framing the oval of her face. Her skin was as smooth and unlined, her nose was as straight and as short, the smudge of freckles as faint across the upper part of her cheek – but her brown eyes weren't as warm and soft as he remembered, and there was an unremembered hardness to her mouth.

It had been a long time since he had last come to Moorside.

Even as he stared at her, lost, she relented somewhat. She rose from her knees.

'While you're thinking of an answer,' she said more softly, 'I'll get you some coffee. It seems to me that you need it.'

Why had he come? He tried to tell her, over the dark brown coffee that she gave him, deliberately avoiding her eyes as he did so. He tried to tell her of the anger that Potter's words had caused him and she broke in—

'It doesn't matter. We know it was over a long time ago.'

He tried to tell her that he had felt the need to speak to her after the inquest to explain why he hadn't objected to Potter's statements and she insisted—

'It's of no *consequence*, Peter.'

So he had to come to his depression and the reasons for it, Stephen Sainsby's words, the whisky—

'...and I wanted to see you. Simple as that. Don't know why. Wanted to see you, be here in this room, where I used to feel warm and, well, happy. I wanted to talk with you and hear music – I even brought some tapes over – and drive out the image of ... of...'

Wordlessly, Shirley took the tapes out of the paper bag, and selected one. A few minutes later from the tape-recorder in the corner of the room came a Sinatra song, slow and vibrant. Shirley sat in the chair opposite him and sipped her coffee. Her eyes were fixed on his. He couldn't read what they said.

He finished the coffee. 'Songs for Swingin' Lovers' swirled around him. Shirley sat there, staring at him.

'I have the uncomfortable feeling,' he said eventually, 'that you don't even see me.'

She smiled faintly.

'I see you, Peter, but clearly, for the first time since we met.'

'I don't understand.'

'You came here to-night because you remembered this as a place where you were warm and happy, wasn't that what you said? What did you leave unsaid? Let me tell you. You came back here because you were down. Because you wanted a sympathetic shoulder to cry on. You came back hoping that things would be as they were. Hoping that you only had to walk in through the door for the months in between to be forgotten. I used to think you were sensitive and thoughtful, but now I see you as a selfish, egocentric boor. I sit here and I look at you and think of you as you were – as I thought you were – but it's all overlaid with the image that you now present. Half drunk, hardly coherent, and expecting me to fall into bed with you the moment you feel desire coming on.'

The tones of her voice were even and measured. They held no rancour. The words didn't nettle him. Perhaps she was right. But he didn't think so. Even though some of her criticism was justified.

'I never came round here again, after Jean-nette came back,' he said slowly.

'Quite right,' she agreed.

'And I didn't telephone or write.'

'I didn't expect you to, after the first week.'

'I'm sorry.'

He looked steadily at her.

'I'm indifferent,' she shrugged. 'It hurt then – not now. It's been over for some time now, and your coming here to-night was a mistake.'

'Yes.'

But her coolness nettled him somewhat. Deliberately he left her and walked through to the small kitchen to take down two tumblers.

'To celebrate the end of a friendship,' he said coldly.

'Not for me, thanks,' she replied, equally coldly.

Her glass remained untouched while he took a long drink.

'I'm equally indifferent to you getting drunk – as long as you don't do it here.'

Peter ignored the remark, and took another drink.

'You've described me as an egocentric boor,' he said, 'so I might as well behave like one. I'm going to tell you the story of my life – at least, my life with Jeannette and–'

'Peter–'

He raised his hand, staring at her a little owlishly.

'I know what you're going to say. It's of no consequence to you. All right, I accept that. The fact remains that I've got something to remove from my system and I'm going to try to do it. You, perforce, will be my audience. You say you know why I came here to-night – I'm not convinced that you were right or fair in what you said. I certainly needed to apologise – I've done so, I am doing so. But I also need to explain – and the fact that you don't want to hear is irrelevant. I'm that ego-centric.'

Peter took another drink. He felt a little lightheaded. Shirley sat quietly, with her hands in her lap, staring at him. Her eyes were very bright.

'There's only one word for the way Jeannette came into my life. She swept in. I was knocked clean off my feet – indeed, if you bear in mind the fact that she was always capable of bowling me over you'll appreciate what happened later more clearly.

'I married her within three weeks of our meeting. She was bright, beautiful and vivacious, with traditional blue eyes and long blonde hair – but I needn't describe her, you knew her. Why did she marry me, though? Boredom, security? – I don't think so. I believe she was genuinely fond of me, perhaps in love with me, for a while. But I couldn't live her sort of life. She wanted gaiety, and parties, and sudden impulsive trips. She was an expensive woman to keep and my junior partnership was not *that* remunerative. I did my best to increase the firm's profits, and I even did some speculating.'

Peter stopped suddenly, staring into his glass. He thought of Sam Gaines's words and he shivered.

'But arguments developed,' he hurried on, turning away from Shirley, 'particularly when I came home some days to find she'd arranged a party at the drop of a hat. After one particular incident – the details of which I won't bore you with, but it was quite a slanging match – she charged out of the house in what is described as high dudgeon. I thought that she would cool off, and return the next day. She did, when I was out. But only to pack her things. I didn't see her or hear from her for seven months.'

He turned to face Shirley. She nodded.

'That's where I came in,' she said softly. 'I … I think I will take that drink after all.'

He watched her sip at the glass.

'I didn't want to hurt you, Shirley.'

'Forget it.'

'I didn't even want to start an affair with you – it just happened. You remember how I'd seen you working in the library a couple of times and we'd met accidentally at the country club and how that clown Edwards was causing trouble. You remember that my impulse to take you home wasn't a planned thing at all and then–'

'I remember,' she said flatly.

'Yes.'

Peter sat down morosely, pouring himself another drink. The bottle was looking the worse for wear.

'I didn't get in touch, or try to do so, with Jeannette. She'd left me, she'd made her decision and well, I admit, with the way I was working and the pleasure I took in your company, I was living very much for the day, each day, with no thought to the future.'

'You were well set up. A job, a girl-friend, and a wife in the background who could conveniently be forgotten.'

'It wasn't like that,' he flashed, 'and you know it. All right, my pride was hurt when she left me, and I worked hard to get her out of my mind. I was succeeding, and with you–'

'Spare me the details.'

'You've become cynical.'

'It becomes me.'

'It doesn't.'

Silence fell between them.

'Anyway,' she said suddenly, 'it all changed when she came back.'

'I had just dropped you home here, and when I got back there she was, hanging her clothes in the wardrobe. I was stunned. I'd almost forgotten the way she was, the way she looked. And there she was.'

'And there I wasn't.'

'Shirley, I'm sorry. I should have seen you, or written. If the truth be known I was afraid. Jeannette had always been able to do as she willed with me: I loved her and she used it. I still love her, Shirley, I've always loved her – you must realise that. I didn't want to lose her again: I only once asked her where she had been and what she'd been doing when she was away during those seven months. She laughed, and I didn't pursue it. I wanted her back.'

'Thanks.'

'It was no reflection on our relationship,' he said slowly. 'I'm only trying to be objective and honest about it. I was very fond of you, Shirley. But Jeannette always had me, tight.'

'And now she's dead, and you come running – I'm sorry, Peter. I shouldn't have said that.'

It didn't matter. Nothing mattered. Jeannette *was* dead. And nothing he could say would change that, and nothing he could say or do would change the way in which he had behaved towards Shirley, or justify that behaviour. She deserved better than a whining weakling like Peter Marlin, an indecisive, amoral coward who couldn't even see straight at the moment. Whisky-soaked.

Time he went. Time he wasn't here. Apologise once more, say something grandiose like you'll never see me again and walk out into the night. Trouble was, difficulty in rising.

'Peter, are you all right?'

'Of course.'

He was upright. But his words had been slurred. Shirley was standing too, but her features were blurred.

'Shirley–'

He put out a hand. He wanted to say he was sorry, that he was going. But he felt a heat rising through his veins. He could hardly breathe and his heart was hammering violently. He was rocking, lurching on his feet. Briefly he felt her shoulder under his hand, then he was falling...

It was the dawn chorus that woke him. He was lying on the settee, fully clothed but for his jacket and shoes. Light filtered dimly through closed curtains. His head felt like a football, solidly kicked on numerous occasions. He remembered. Whisky, no lunch, headache powders and more, a lot more, whisky. He swore.

On the chair he saw Shirley's dress. The shoulder was torn. He must have caught at it as he fell. He rose painfully, and began to make his way towards the bedroom. He stopped. Things were better as they were. There was nothing more to be said.

When he left the bungalow he closed the door behind him, softly. The light click carried an air of finality.

CHAPTER II

1

A hot shower, a shave, a complete change of clothes and several strong cups of coffee made Peter a new man. It was a clear sunny morning and his spirits lifted somewhat: thoughts of Jeannette receded, and while he still felt pangs of conscience for his behaviour towards Shirley the previous evening, these too he stifled. He had other things to worry about. By seven o'clock he was hard at work on the Noble and Harris file.

He arrived at Greygables punctually at ten. The house was a pretentious one, but he liked it for all that. The long curving drive was flanked by mountain ash, laurel and rhododendron, above which the grey gables, for which the house was named, loomed stolidly and unemotionally. The Gothic nature of the house appealed to him, in spite of its flamboyance and the accretions, hideous in their nonconformity, which had been built at one side to furnish living accommodation for the cars that the Gaines family possessed.

One of them was in the drive now – the Jaguar. Its offside wing was almost torn off.

Beside it stood the slight, grey-haired form of Mrs Gaines, leather gloved, planting trowel in one hand. When he drew up short of the Jaguar she turned, shading her old eyes against the morning sun.

It was an affectation. Mrs Gaines had eyes that were far from weak: they had the ability to pierce through humbug and prevarication. It was always best to tell the truth to Mrs Gaines.

'Good morning, Mr Marlin.'

He had been her solicitor since he had come to Martin and Sainsby and she had known him as a boy, earlier. Sometimes she treated him as though he were still the scruffy child she had known. Perhaps she had a right to do so, for Peter's father had once worked for her, on the farm across the meadows.

'Good-morning, Mrs Gaines. You're looking well.'

'The Jaguar isn't. Samuel's doing. It's always my hope that one of these days he will learn the value of property – and of money. It's a good thing–'

She checked herself, and he was aware of her hesitation. One does not discuss one's hopes with the hired help – even if he happens to be a solicitor and trustee to the holdings from which a large part of one's income is derived.

'You'll be driving with him to the meeting,

I imagine.'

Peter nodded assent.

'Mr Marlin, tell me – what is going to happen there this morning?'

'I think that Amalgamated Industries Ltd. will acquire a controlling interest in Noble and Harris Ltd.'

'With the support of our vote,' said Mrs Gaines, watching him keenly.

'Yes.'

She turned away, casually.

'And what do we hope to get out of it, Mr Marlin?'

'A great deal of money, Mrs Gaines, possibly even in the short term.'

'I'm delighted to hear it. Might help pay for that offside wing.'

It was Sam Gaines. He slammed the door behind him as he came out of the house and down the steps. There was a wide grin on his tanned features, and the fair hair that flopped forward across his forehead gave him a boyish look. He was thirty-three, and emotionally immature.

'Never fear, Mother,' he smiled, taking the trowel from her hand and touching her fingers slightly with his lips. 'I will look after the inheritance. The vast battalions of commerce shall be vanquished before the swift erudition of my mind. At least, if Peter will explain it all to me beforehand in monosyllabic terms.'

'It's nice,' commented Mrs Gaines dryly, 'to know that the family fortunes are in such capable hands. It's a pity that those hands don't *drive* more capably.'

It was curious. Mrs Gaines had a formidable reputation in the neighbourhood. She was not a person to cross. She was quick, intelligent and forceful; her assessment of individuals was merciless, her using of them even more so. As a businesswoman she had many years ago shown her mettle when her husband died – but with Sam she was different. Or perhaps it wasn't so curious. He was an only child, and his father *had* died thirty years ago.

It would take them twenty minutes to get to the meeting, so they should make it for a 10.45 start quite easily. But it wasn't a twenty minutes that Peter was looking forward to. Sam was usually easy company, but the questions that Peter was expecting were not long coming.

'Well, respected lawyer friend and succour of the thick, tell me all about it, without prevarication, or words as long as the lawyer's arm. First thing we do, Dick the Butcher had said, let's kill all the lawyers, but Shakespeare was a cynic and I don't feel that way, dear boy. The meeting, what, why, wherefore? Tell me all. In particular, why do we support the takeover?'

'I'd better start from the beginning,' said

Peter slowly.

'Do, dear boy, do!' Sam rolled down the window and a stream of cold air hit Peter in the back of the neck.

'Your father's estate included eight thousand shares in Noble and Harris–'

'The famous textile firm,' yelped Sam to the wind.

'–which are held in trust, the beneficiaries being your mother for life in the first place, and then you after her death.'

'And the trustees for which are now you, me and the senile Mr Byrne of Byrne, Mc-Master and Byrne, Accountants Extraordinary! I'm with you so far, Peter, with you absolutely all the way!'

Peter grunted. Sometimes Sam Gaines was a little too much to take. His high spirits were wearing, particularly since there was much to Sam apart from tomfoolery. There was little to support the suspicion, but Peter felt he was right in the estimate.

'As the holders of eight thousand shares you classify – or the trust does, at least – as minority shareholders. Noble and Harris have an issued capital of thirty thousand £1 shares.'

'Major, minor, who cares while the money rolls in?'

'You'd care, since it's unlikely to continue to roll in, the way things are going,' snapped Peter. 'You'll remember two years ago I told you and Byrne that I was unhappy about the firm. To say that it was going through a lean time was euphemistic.'

'Steady, Peter, watch your language!'

'You'll remember,' continued Peter doggedly, 'that we all went to see the board, and told them that the trust was far from satisfied with the return yielded by the shares. We expressed that dissatisfaction at the annual general meeting.'

'And the attitude of the board was – ah – hostile. I remember, I do indeed.'

'I talked things over with your mother, and suggested that we buy all the outstanding shares in the company in the hope that we could improve the position. We couldn't agree, and you supported your mother's point of view.'

'Peter, you don't know what you're saying! How could I resist a dear, old, grey-haired lady?'

'Well, things haven't improved. And now, Amalgamated Industries are stepping in.'

'But why should we support, and vote for, the takeover?'

Some of the banter had gone.

'If we had bought the shares for the trust we could have exercised control over the company activities and – well, we didn't, so that is that. Amalgamated Industries want to take over. This means one of two things. Either they intend to pump more capital into the firm, and expand it, diversify, make it a going concern, or they intend to reorganise it and capitalise upon some of the fixed assets. A sale of the premises in Swindon, for instance, could bring in a quick return, and there's also the whole question of the subsidiary in New Zealand...'

'You're losing me, lad.'

'Either way, the trust is bound to benefit. Amalgamated Industries will be doing for the trust, what the trustees weren't prepared to do for themselves. That's why I have recommended that the takeover be supported.'

For a while there was only the sound of the wind whipping through the open window, above the muted roar of the engine. Peter felt Sam's grey eyes watching him carefully.

'You're pretty keen on the whole thing – you're *sold,* aren't you, Peter?'

'I'm sold on it,' agreed Peter simply. 'The trust will benefit.'

'But what do *you* get out of it, Peter?'

Peter went cold. Stiffly, he asked, 'What do you mean?'

'Well, here you are, working up a sweat over this takeover – I mean you've done a hell of a lot of work on it, I know. I was talking to Joan Shaw the other day and she told me the files you have on Noble and Harris are nobody's business–'

Peter shot him a quick glance.

'Joan had no right to discuss office affairs outside the–'

'Peter,' soothed Gaines, 'it's all trust holding stuff. *Isn't it?*'

'It is,' replied Peter grimly. His hands were tight on the wheel.

'There you are, then.' Sam Gaines smiled expansively. 'What was the harm? But as I was saying, you've sweated blood over all this – but I don't understand. After all, what do *you* get out of it?'

'The first duty of a trustee,' snapped Peter, 'is to direct his best efforts towards the trust. As a professional trustee it's my professional duty to do that, and use all the skill and knowledge at my command to–'

'Okay, okay,' yelped Gaines in a falsetto, 'I'm convinced! Put on the handcuffs – I'll go quietly.'

'For God's sake, don't you ever stop clowning?'

'Sometimes,' smiled Gaines. 'Sometimes, when it's necessary, Peter. But then, who's to know when I'm clowning?'

Precisely, thought Peter grimly, as he swung the car into the reserved parking space in front of the factory and offices of Noble and Harris (Textiles) Ltd.

There were fifteen people in the board-room: eight comprised the board of directors, with Charles Shaw-Lefevre in the chair. Apart from Peter and Sam Gaines, representing the trust holding, there were four other shareholders.

The fifteenth man present was sitting quietly down at the end of the table. His face was thin and intelligent, his hairline high and thinning; long sensitive fingers sat silently on the table, lightly resting on a thick file.

To Sam's inquiry, Peter answered, 'Paul Jackson.'

'I thought you didn't know him?'

Peter met Sam's gaze carefully.

'We know everyone else in the room,' he commented quietly. 'Who else could *he* be?'

Sam grinned widely, and took his seat.

Shaw-Lefevre was pompous and socially something of a buffoon but he was an efficient chairman. He announced the calling of an extraordinary general meeting and read the notice convening the meeting. Briefly he explained the purpose of the meeting – to consider the offer made by Amalgamated Industries Ltd. for the purchase of the shares in Noble and Harris Ltd.

'Your agenda contains all the details required by the Companies Act. I will simply add and emphasise that if you decide to accept the offer the choice is open to you to accept a cash payment for your shares, or to accept in payment shares in Amalgamated Industries Ltd. We recommend that the offer be accepted, and will issue a written recommendation which will also disclose our holdings, state our intention, as directors, to accept, and state all other relevant interests and information required by the Acts. Before I put the resolution to the meeting I would ask if there are any questions or points arising.'

'Bejabers,' muttered Sam from the corner of his mouth, 'they're railroading this through.' He leaned forward. Peter waited apprehensively. 'Mr Chairman. I note the presence among us of a stranger – to wit, the gentleman there, whom I presume to be Mr Jackson. I would like some information upon where he fits into the picture, if at all.'

Shaw-Lefevre frowned.

'It's all in the papers, Mr Gaines.'

'Nevertheless...' prompted Sam with a smile.

'Hrrumph. Yes. Well, if the offer is accepted by the shareholders – who are all present – Mr Jackson will be a member of a reconstituted board, this being one of the terms of the takeover.'

'And the board will consist of...?' inquired Sam sweetly.

'That is not – if I may, Mr Chairman–' interrupted Paul Jackson smoothly – 'that is not yet decided, of course, but Mr Shaw-Lefevre will be a member of the new board and I can assure you that Noble and Harris will not be entirely swallowed up – indeed, they will remain a distinct entity quite apart from my firm, Amalgamated Industries Ltd. And I can also assure you that all those shareholders who take shares in my firm by way of payment will be more than adequately improving their shareholding properties.'

'And just who,' asked Gaines carefully, 'is Amalgamated Industries Ltd?'

There was a short silence. Jackson raised a thin, affected eyebrow.

'I beg your pardon? I'm sorry, Mr Chairman...'

'Mr Gaines,' commented Shaw-Lefevre heavily, 'is perhaps unacquainted with the Companies Register. Details may be discovered therein. Are there any other questions?'

'Just one.' Sam jumped in unabashed. 'How does Mr Jackson hope to improve our holdings?'

Shaw-Lefevre looked somewhat uncomfortable, but glanced towards Jackson. The file lay open under Jackson's long fingers.

'If you wish to accept a cash payment for your shares, Mr Gaines,' remarked Jackson quietly, 'you will receive £4 10s per share. From the figures that I have that is probably about four times the price at which they were acquired by your trust holding. Even allowing for depreciation in the value of money, you will be well compensated there. You may feel, however, that you would do better to take our shares instead. That is your decision. I would perhaps also agree with you if you were to suggest that the price of £4 10s which we are offering is a high one. However, my board feels that there is probably quite a lot of asset value in Noble and Harris. We feel that, if you will forgive me, Mr Chairman, we may well be able, by better management or by liquidation, to make the shares worth a great deal more than this quoted price. We feel, for instance, that present conditions in New Zealand are such that a sale of the interest there could be effected at considerable profit – and perhaps some of the English holdings could yet produce a higher profit. I cannot, and will not, enter any commitment, of course, but I can assure you that the price is more than fair, and the prospects are more than favourable.'

'And I and my board,' added Shaw-Lefevre with emphasis, 'are persuaded by Mr Jackson's arguments and intend to accept the offer. May I now move the formal resolution?'

'By all means,' waved Sam airily. Someone down the table glowered, and Sam added cheerily to him, 'For my part at least, old boy.'

He turned to Peter. 'I don't like Jackson,' he whispered with a smile. 'He hath a villain's cheek. There is something here which smells.'

'Sam, listen. I've gone over his figures closely. I agree with what Jackson has in mind. I reckon that this time next year will see a distribution of a capital bonus amounting to £3 a share. I think we should accept the offer.'

The appeal to Gaines's cupidity was not wasted, as Peter suspected it would not be.

'I'm relying on your advice, dear friend,' muttered Sam. 'I'll go along.'

The votes were necessary. Although the trust holding was a minority holding and voted with the board, the four other shareholders voted against the resolution. They were unsuccessful in their opposition.

As Peter made his way out at the conclusion of the meeting, Sam caught at his shoulder.

'I didn't realise it was going to be so close. Why did those four vote against? If we had voted that way too the motion would have been lost. What did *they* know that we didn't?'

'Nothing,' said Peter emphatically. 'They're all members of the Noble family. They don't possess an ounce of business acumen. They believe in tradition.'

'And you don't.'

'Only if it pays dividends.'

They emerged into the sunlight. Sam stopped at the top of the steps above the car park.

'I need a drag.'

As he stood there lighting his cigarette Peter strolled on down the stairs ahead of him casually. At the bottom of the steps he turned to look back. Paul Jackson was hurrying down the steps past Sam, briefcase in his hand. As he drew level with Peter his eyes flickered up: they carried a glint of triumph.

When Peter drove from the car park he was acutely aware that Sam could have noted the glance which had passed between them.

2

Through the frosted glass panel of the door to Joan's office Peter could make out two figures. He opened the door and Bill Daly swung around to him. His thick bull neck was red and there was anger in his handsome face. Joan's colour was heightened also, and Peter could see that they had been arguing about something. They fell silent as he entered.

'You waiting to see me, Bill?'

'Er … no, Mr Marlin, I … er … I just brought the Larkway conveyance in to Joan and she…'

'Did old Larkway finally get round to completion, then?'

'He did,' commented Daly eagerly, as

though glad of the opportunity to justify his presence in Joan's office. 'I thought that he was going to back out again at the last moment, but–'

'Fine,' interrupted Peter. 'Anything for me, Joan?'

'Yes, Mr Marlin, I'll bring it in, in just a moment.'

As Peter closed the door of his own office behind him he smiled to himself. The tone in Joan's voice clearly illustrated that her argument with Bill, whatever it was over, was concluded as far as she was concerned.

He wondered briefly just what it *was* about. Probably some matter of office routine, or crossed lines of responsibility. And yet ... he allowed his mind to dwell briefly on the picture they had presented as he came in to the office. Bill had been leaning with his hands on Joan's desk, arguing. She had been sitting bolt upright, with anger and embarrassment chasing across her face. She looked even prettier when she was angry...

A personal quarrel? Something unconnected with work? Could be – there had been something strained about the silence that had fallen on his entry. But Bill was married; seven years married to a local girl. Peter seemed to remember hearing recently that Mrs Daly was expecting her second child soon. He recalled meeting Mrs Daly once. A small, dowdy woman who should make better of her appearance.

Still, it was all none of his business.

He heard Joan's discreet tap on the door, and a moment later she entered.

'These three letters came this morning: I've drafted replies to two of them.'

He knew that he would simply have to sign them: they would be in order. Joan knew her job.

'The third asks you to get in touch with Mr Corey at the Old Mill. There were two telephone calls. Both gentlemen said they would ring back.'

'That's fine, Joan. Look, I'll sign these at once and then you can get them in the post this afternoon. Now, there was something I wanted you to do ... ah yes, the Blair will. You remember Mrs Blair?'

'At Cardington.'

'Yes. Look, I think the document can now be taken over to her for explanation, and signature. Bill can do that. Perhaps you'd like to drive out with him, and then you two can act as witnesses to the signature. It'll give you a chance to get out of the office for an hour or so, and it's a pleasant drive.'

'I've got rather a lot of work to do, Mr Marlin. Perhaps you could send one of the juniors.'

Peter looked up in surprise.

'Can't it wait? It's a nice afternoon, and I'd

thought you'd welcome the chance to drive across to Cardington.'

'I'd just as soon stay here,' Joan said firmly. 'With your permission I'll ask Betty to go.'

Peter eyed her thoughtfully. Perhaps she didn't want to spend an hour in the car with Bill. He shrugged.

'Up to you, Joan.'

She stood hesitantly at the desk facing him.

'Did everything go all right this morning?' she queried.

'Ahuh. I think the takeover will go through. The files are in my briefcase – perhaps you'll stick them back in the drawer.'

Automatically, Joan reached for the briefcase. Her hand brushed against his, lightly. She still made no move to leave.

'Mr Marlin,' she said finally, in a quiet voice. 'I've said nothing before...'

'Yes...'

'About ... the last few weeks. Well, I'd just like you to know that I'm sorry about the whole thing, and, well, you know.'

He knew. It had been rather pleasant, really, in view of all the condolences, often prying, that he had received, that Joan had said nothing but simply had carried on – not as though nothing had happened, but at least as though there were other things to think about.

'That's very nice of you, Joan. I've appreciated your own sensitivity in the matter.'

'I – I've also heard about the … discussion in Mr Stephen's room yesterday. I gather that you will be leaving the firm, Mr Marlin.'

Peter stared at his hands.

'It is rather more than probable.'

'Have you decided what to do then? Will you be setting up in practice elsewhere? In some other town, perhaps?'

There was a strange eagerness in her tone that he couldn't fathom.

'I really haven't thought about it,' he replied, somewhat puzzled.

'You see,' she said slowly, 'when you leave, I will probably leave the firm also.'

'Why on earth should you do that?'

Her eyes were fixed on his and she was breathing somewhat quickly, and nervously.

'Well, I've been working with you now for some years, and if I may say so, I've got used to you – and you've got used to me – and I think that I would just as soon leave the same time as you. And perhaps – perhaps join your firm when you are established.'

'But Joan,' he protested, 'I've not even thought about what I should do yet. Everything's happened so quickly – I've just not got round to making even the most tentative plans. But I don't understand. Don't you like working with the firm?'

She was silent for a moment. Her eyes were grey-green: he'd never noticed before.

Grey-green … and serious, with an under-lying message for him that emphasised the meaning of her next words.

'I *have* been extremely happy working here,' she said. 'But when you leave, there'll be nothing to keep me here.'

He hoped that he managed to keep the surprise out of his face. There was no mis-taking her meaning. His male egotism was flattered by what she was saying, but the situation was difficult – if not impossible.

Nor was it a situation that he wanted. It added yet another complication to his life. And yet … her lips were slightly parted, and there was a slight flush to her cheek. He had always thought her more than decorative…

With a deliberate effort he kept his voice impersonal.

'I couldn't have wished for a better secre-tary, Joan, nor could I get a better one. But I haven't decided what I'll be doing yet. If you *do* leave the firm, and I need a secretary, I'll certainly employ you. But in view of the uncertainty at the moment, I think you'd be best advised to hang on here.'

He knew that he had mishandled it, but the words were out and they were cold and unfriendly in their tone and in their dis-regard of what she was really saying. They told her that he knew what she had been driving at – she had made her meaning clear enough – but that he was unprepared to accept a relationship with her other than the purely professional one they had enjoyed up to this moment.

She handled the situation far better than he.

'I see, Mr Marlin,' she said softly, and with dignity. 'I'll get these papers filed away at once.'

But after she had closed the door behind her he was still remembering the hurt look in her eyes. It was strange: for him, Joan Shaw had always possessed a sophistication and a professional, efficient approach to life that had made him feel that she would be incapable of being hurt. The memory of the look in her eyes told him now how wrong he was.

The afternoon, which had started badly, continued in the same vein. He had occasion to go through Joan's office twice during the next hour and each time he was aware of a strained, brightly cheerful attitude between them. It irritated him, for he felt very much in the wrong. At one point he thought that he even ought to apologise and perhaps suggest they meet for a drink that evening to talk the matter out.

It was a thought he angrily rejected. He'd never given Joan any encouragement and he was annoyed that she should now put him in this position. It wasn't that he didn't find her attractive – he did. But – there were too many buts, and he didn't intend to analyse them.

His mood blackened as the afternoon wore on.

It was four-thirty, and the end of a Land Commission problem on his desk, that left him completely vulnerable to the surprise of an unexpected telephone call.

The intercom buzzed and Joan's cool voice said, 'Mr Marlin, there's a call for you. It's Miss Walker. Shall I put her through?'

'Miss Walker?'

'Shall I put her through?'

Somewhat dazed, Peter hurriedly agreed. A moment later Shirley's husky voice was at the end of the line.

'Peter? I must apologise for ringing you like this at the office. Something's happened and I thought you should know about it. I rang you this morning but you were out … Peter?'

'Yes, yes, I'm still here. It's just that I was taken a little aback, hearing your voice. You were saying?'

There was a short silence.

'As I said, I'm sorry to ring you like this. But I received a visit this afternoon. From the police.'

'The police! But–'

'It was all very unpleasant. I was questioned … about you, and about Jeannette. Various inferences were drawn.'

'I don't understand.'

'They know that you spent last night here, Peter.'

The watch on Peter's wrist sounded inordinately loud. Among the violent, whirling thoughts in his mind was an irrelevant one – had Joan left the line open in her office?

'I don't understand. Why should they come to see you about me and Jeannette? I've answered enough of their blasted questions and so have you. Why again, now?'

'Not they – there was just one man. A new man. An Inspector Crow. He's been called in, from Scotland Yard, apparently.'

'There's enough stuff on the whole thing down at the station,' Peter protested, 'to make it unnecessary for any further badgering to go on. And there's certainly no need for them to bother you!'

'I think that your appearance at my house last night has led them to think otherwise.'

'Shirley,' Peter said urgently. 'I'm sorry – it's my fault – I didn't apologise last night, nor this morning – but I do so now. I've behaved like a fool, and a coward, and worse. But this – leave it with me. I'll get on to this at once.'

He hesitated.

'Shall I ring you again – to let you know the outcome?'

In the long pause that followed he almost thought that she had left the phone. When she finally replied her voice was low, but controlled.

'I don't think that will be necessary.'

He sat there dully for several minutes after she rang off. Then the anger returned and he reached for the intercom, to ask Joan to get the police station for him.

It was unnecessary. Her voice came to him first.

'Mr Marlin, there's a gentleman in the outer office who wishes to see you.'

She paused.

'He gives his name as Inspector Crow.'

3

He was skeletal.

In Peter's experience there were occasionally men whose names summed up their appearance. Inspector Crow was one of them. He was over six feet in height, but could have weighed little more than nine or ten stone. His dark suit was well cut but hung on his thin frame carelessly. His domed head was hairless, his eyes deep-sunk, heavy-browed, his prominent nose jutted out from fleshless cheeks. From bony wrists were suspended narrow hands and thin, long fingers.

But his eyes were young and lively, and he was not without a sense of humour.

'You seem surprised at my appearance …

in your office, Mr Marlin.' The voice also possessed a youthful quality. 'May I sit down?'

Peter came to himself.

'Please do, Inspector Crow. Yes … your visit is opportune. I was about to ring you at the station.'

'To complain?'

'I see no reason why you should have bothered Miss Walker.'

'Or yourself.'

'As you say.'

Inspector Crow smiled thinly. 'I feel sad that I have to differ, Mr Marlin, but perhaps I should explain the situation. You see I have been called in to assist the local police in the investigation into your wife's death and while I have every confidence in their individual and collective ability in general matters my experience forces me to presuppose that the best way of obtaining relevant information is to get it myself, in person.'

'This is nonsense. It means that we have to go through the whole thing again.'

'Not precisely so, Mr Marlin. I have already read through the reports and voluminous material assiduously collected by the local police engaged on the case – there are just a few points of detail I need to acquaint myself with, and a few people to see. Like yourself–'

'And Miss Walker?'

'And Miss Walker.'

'I don't understand why you feel it necessary to subject her to further questioning.'

Inspector Crow spread his bony hands. 'One never knows what may be found. It is in questioning people that one sometimes finds activation for the crime, for instance.'

Peter stared at him in astonishment.

'You surely don't suspect *me* of murdering my wife?'

Crow was looking at him quizzically, and Peter realised the inference in the involuntary remark that he had made.

'They were your words, Mr Marlin,' commented Crow quietly.

'There is nothing between me and Miss Walker,' said Peter doggedly. 'It was over a long time ago – when my wife returned.'

'Yes ... and last night?'

'There is nothing between Miss Walker and myself. I have no doubt she will have already explained what happened last night.'

'Quite adequately.'

Inspector Crow's eyes watched him lazily.

'Would you like to give me a brief account of your movements the evening of your wife's death, Mr Marlin?'

'I would not. It's on record already but in the circumstances, Inspector, I'll repeat myself. I was working late here at the office – a fact that Miss Shaw will verify–'

'Ah yes, Miss Shaw...'

'–and when I left here, at nine-thirty, I locked up.'

'Miss Shaw had left previously?'

'Yes. I then–'

'Did you see Miss Shaw leave?'

'No, I didn't.'

'Did you see her at the office that evening?'

'No.'

'How is it that she saw you but you did not see her?'

Peter sighed patiently.

'My office is on the first floor. Miss Shaw works in the ante-room to my office. Directly outside her door are the stairs leading to the second floor. At the top of the flight is a glass-panelled door leading into the room where we keep all our bound copies of statutes and law reports. They are too bulky and numerous to be kept in the offices, of course.'

'Of course.'

'On the evening in question I had gone up to the library to look up some authorities on a case that I had to prepare for counsel. I was stuck in there all evening. It would seem that Joan Shaw was also working late, though I didn't realise it at the time. She saw the light in the library, and she saw my shadow on the glass. She would have known if I had left the library for I would have had to come down the stairs and past her office.'

'Yes. She had made the point in her statement, as I remember.'

'Then why bother me again? All I can say is that she saw me here, and the times she gives in her statement make it obvious that I am telling the truth when I say I left here and drove straight home to find my house in darkness – and my wife dead.'

'In the sitting-room.'

The gaunt frame of Inspector Crow hunched forward as he prodded Peter for more details – then abruptly he changed his line of questioning.

'Tell me about your wife – when she was alive, I mean.'

It was all familiar, painful ground. Peter Marlin frowned.

'She was young, beautiful, vivacious – and I was far too dull for her. We quarrelled a great deal. I loved her.'

'And she left you.'

'Yes.'

'Only to return to you again after ... what was it ... seven months?'

'Almost to the day.'

Crow raised bushy eyebrows.

'And what sort of existence did you two lead thereafter?'

'We lived – as the coroner put it – reasonably amicably after that.'

'In spite of Miss Walker.'

'Jeannette knew about it.'

'Yes.'

'Her return ended it.'

'Yes.'

'I'm a busy man, Inspector Crow.'

'And a very succinct one, Mr Marlin.'

'It comes of a great deal of questioning. Answers become stock ones.'

Inspector Crow smiled and his deep-sunk eyes looked happy.

'But faces reflect feelings, and character, that words do not, Mr Marlin. Which is one reason why I came to see you – and Miss Walker.'

He rose to his feet.

'However, that will do for now. I thank you for the brief minutes you have given me. They've been instructive. Er ... you never discovered where your wife went, when she left you?'

'No. It was of no consequence. She returned.'

'I agree. We have looked into the matter closely. It was of no consequence.'

At the door his skeletal figure paused.

'I hear you may soon be leaving this firm, Mr Marlin.' His smile was as benign as his narrow features would allow. 'Please remain in touch with us.'

'Why?'

It was a stupid question. Inspector Crow was no longer smiling.

'Because there is much in this investigation that puzzles me. And I would hate to lose touch with one of the major actors in the scenario. It has been a pleasure to meet you, Mr Marlin – but just one more favour. May I take up a little of your secretary's time?'

'Be my guest,' said Peter coldly.

Inspector Crow disappeared into the outer office. Peter sat down. He felt strangely uneasy. It was an uncomfortable feeling that was not dispelled by his telling himself that he had nothing to worry about.

And this in itself was worrying.

4

By five-thirty Peter was acutely depressed. He made little attempt to analyse the reasons for his depression; he was aware that it was only partly caused by the questioning of Inspector Crow, and the re-emergence of all the anxiety surrounding Jeannette's death. There was also Shirley's call – and the coolness of her tone. Yet she had taken the trouble to ring him, and warn him. That must mean something. Her final words had been pretty final, nevertheless.

Five-thirty. He realised that he had been sitting here in the leather chair for forty-five minutes, saying nothing, seeing nothing, doing nothing. He had a slight headache. Time to go home.

Home... Perhaps it would be a good thing, after all, to leave the firm. He could get away from this town and the house and its memories. Maybe he could start his own firm, somewhere else: life could well be a little difficult to begin with, but things would sort themselves out in time.

And if he wanted a good secretary, he could rely on Joan to join him.

The thought was a stupid one. He could never employ Joan now.

He rose and walked through to the outer office. Joan had gone. It was unlike her, really, to leave before he did, without first popping her head round the door to discover if there was anything urgent he required, and if not to wish him good night.

But there were reasons for her conduct now.

He stuck his hands in his pockets and walked down the stairs. As he came down he heard voices below, at the entrance to the building. When he came into sight of the door he found himself looking at John Sainsby's back. He had just taken leave of someone. A client, probably.

Then, as Peter approached the doorway, John turned. His face was pale, his mouth loose with worry. He gave a start of surprise as he saw Peter.

'Oh! I didn't hear you coming, Peter.'

'Are you all right?'

John Sainsby nodded quickly and nervously. He forced a ghastly half-smile to his narrow features.

'Of course. You just leaving?'

Peter nodded, his eyes on the street. There was a man crossing from Green Street into the High. It was an unmistakable figure: tall, thin, with a domed head. What had Inspector Crow been talking to John Sainsby about?

'You don't look well, John. Are you sure you're feeling all right?'

'Quite sure.'

The answer was too quick and too jerky. Peter eyed him with concern.

'Why don't you join me for a drink? We could walk along to the Bull: it'll be open by the time we get there, and a bit of fresh air, followed by a stiff whisky, will do us both good.'

Sainsby hesitated. Then, impulsively, he said, 'I think that's a good idea. Let's go.'

As they walked along the High Street there was little opportunity to talk. The pavement was crowded. Once or twice John was forced to move on ahead and Peter observed that some of the precision of his walk seemed to have deserted him.

'It's a long time since I found myself the first customer of the evening in a pub,' Peter said as he placed the whisky and lime in front of his companion. He was thinking that

81

it was a curiously effeminate drink that John had asked for. But it was treated effeminately: John swallowed it in a quick gulp. Peter stared.

'The evening will be an expensive one,' he grinned. 'I trust you feel better?'

Sainsby smiled lop-sidedly.

'I'll get a couple more,' he said, and left for the bar. When he returned, he seemed to have regained some of his normal composure.

'I imagine you'll have received the notice of dissolution of the partnership, Peter.'

'This afternoon.'

Sainsby shrugged unhappily.

'I'm only sorry that I couldn't do anything about it. The old man was adamant. Not that it matters anyway.'

'From which I gather that you're still thinking about this Bar nonsense.'

'Not nonsense, Peter. Not thinking, either. Decided.'

Peter sipped his drink thoughtfully.

'I think you're nuts. The practice is going well. Stephen will retire in a few years, if not sooner. Depending on his political kites. You'll be senior partner, with a couple of juniors. And you're thinking of giving it up—'

'Decided.'

'All right, you've decided to give it up for a career at the Bar. You know what you're doing? Hell, it means you've got to read for

Bar Finals to start with, and you've not done any academic law since Law School. That's going to take a year at least: I trust I'm not being over-sanguine! And then there's pupillage – and although there's more work around these days for the barrister who's just starting his career, it still costs money while you work for the exams and devil for your senior. It can be a long haul. And while you're reasonably well known around here, you know damn' well there are no chambers in the vicinity, and you'll have to make new contacts and all that – you're nuts, John. Think it over.'

Sainsby shook his head.

'No. I know what I'm doing. Things...'

He looked at Peter oddly for a moment, as though he were about to say something. He checked himself.

'I know what I'm doing,' he insisted stubbornly.

Conversation was desultory thereafter. Peter wanted to ask why John had been talking with Crow – the inspector couldn't have spent more than fifteen minutes with Joan, which meant that he must have been closeted with John for almost half an hour. What had they discussed? Peter couldn't think how he could tactfully broach the subject. Sainsby obviously had his problems, and Peter certainly had his. He saw John and himself objectively for a moment: two young men sitting in a pub staring at morose glasses of whisky. They were doing each other no good at all. Sainsby obviously recognised it too.

'Got to be going,' he said suddenly. 'I'll see you tomorrow. Oh, by the way, can you get across to the Holford firm next Tuesday evening? They want one of us along for their annual meeting.'

'Remind me to-morrow, John. I should be able to make it. I've nothing to keep me at home.'

'Er … no,' said Sainsby nervously. 'Well, I'll … er … see you.'

When he'd gone there was only the whisky and his own thoughts. The whisky had already landed him in trouble. Peter left and walked back to the office, and his car.

He took the longer route home, and stopped off at the country club on the way, for a meal. Jeannette had spent more than a few evenings here – with him and without him. When she was there alone he had always picked her up. She had driven no car: she had liked to be driven.

By eight-fifteen he was home. The evening stretched ahead of him and the house was quiet. He tried to read for a while: the *Solicitor's Gazette* first, and then a novel he found in the dining-room. Jeannette had borrowed it from the library. They hadn't yet asked for its return.

He found himself unable to concentrate.

His thoughts kept returning to Inspector Crow. Why had the man found it necessary to see Shirley – and then himself? All right, he was new to the investigation – but why question them like this? It could only mean that in some way suspicion was falling on Peter Marlin, and the motive for murder was Shirley. It was a repeat of the suspicion that had been immediate, after the murder. The local police had seemed almost to assume, without bothering to look farther, that he had been, at the least, involved. It was only when his whereabouts at the time of the murder had become known that they had started to look elsewhere.

But now Inspector Crow was following the same pattern. Jeannette – and Peter and Shirley.

It was all patently absurd. But logical.

Peter got up and prowled around the house.

'It was of no consequence.'

But it had been. Jeannette's going had been agony: her unexplained absence had been hell: her return had been a searing relief and yet a problem in itself.

Where had she been? With whom had she stayed? Inspector Crow's words seemed to have implied that the police had checked and discovered her whereabouts during that period. Or did they?

He found himself in Jeannette's room.

When she had come back she had insisted on using the spare room at the front, fitted out with some new bedroom furniture, and a desk, and typewriter. She had dabbled, unsuccessfully, at short-story writing for women's magazines. The spare room; Jeannette's room... Potter had said that they had lived together reasonably amicably. They had. That was about the only way it could be described, the way they had lived after her return.

He opened her wardrobe. Her clothes were still there. It was as though she were still alive, and when he put his hand in the pocket of her coat it was with a quickened pulse as though she might walk in through the door and catch him in his action. His degrading action.

For he wanted to know, suddenly. Where she had been. Whom she had seen.

But the coat told him nothing. Nor did the rest of her clothes. The police had been through the lot, anyway. And yet, as he remembered, not closely. They had gone over the sitting-room very carefully, and yet when he returned to the house he had received the impression that elsewhere their examination of the rooms had been cursory, desultory.

Peter found himself thinking about Jeannette's desk. It was Victorian, and its ornate carving contained a hidden drawer of the kind so loved by the Victorian paterfamilias. Had the police checked that drawer? Had they asked him about the desk? If they had, he couldn't remember. Was it possible that the drawer had been overlooked?

It couldn't have been. When he inspected the desk he found marks, scratches on the flamboyant bosses. The hidden drawer had been opened – but not with a key. He pushed the polished oak boss aside to expose the keyhole.

He paused. Jeannette had had a key, but he had not seen it since her death. If the police knew about the drawer they would have used the key – *if they had found it* – or they would have asked him about it. They hadn't asked.

The police would not have forced the drawer.

He stared at the scratches then slowly put down one hand and dragged open the drawer – it had a spring activation normally, when opened with a key, but the spring was now broken and obstructing the drawer. Inside, a jumble of paper in an untidy heap. Nothing of any consequence.

Peter stared at it dully. His mind was a blank. He began to push the drawer back, slowly, against the obstructive spring. The drawer refused to move back. Carefully he withdrew it completely and scrabbled to remove the broken spring, then peered into the aperture. There was a small packet at the back, where it had fallen down behind the drawer.

He took it into the sitting-room and stared at it for a long time. It consisted of three letters, taped flatly together.

Finally, he read them.

When he put them down, he felt physically sick.

It was some time before he found himself able to go to the telephone. He heard the ringing sound three times only before the receiver was lifted.

'Shirley? This is Peter. I ... I think I know who murdered Jeannette.'

CHAPTER III

1

'Well?'

Shirley stared helplessly at Peter Marlin, as he sat nervously on the edge of the settee. His entrance to her house this evening had been in marked contrast to his last appearance; this time he had been distraught, upset, hesitant and quite unlike the brash, drunken young man who had intruded recently.

'Well, what do you think?'

When he had spoken to her on the telephone she had been unable to quell the sudden quickening of her pulse at the sound of his voice. Perhaps she would never be able to quell it. Shirley had thought that she could get over the havoc that Peter had caused in her previously ordered existence – she'd thought that she *had* got over it. Until he had reappeared that evening, drunk, falling about the place. She had been as contemptuous of her own emotions that evening as she had been of him, and for that reason she had spoken cuttingly to him. He had got the message then, and yet he seemed to have turned to her now that he had discovered the letters.

She held them in her hand. Impatiently, Peter blurted out,

'Well, don't you think I'm right?'

She shook her head in despair.

'Really, Peter, I don't know. I can understand the shock that these letters must have been. I – I gather that you had no idea that–'

'I had no idea,' he agreed grimly.

She saw a sudden shadow pass over his face as he looked at her and realised intuitively that he was remembering that while he could feel pain now at the thought that his wife had had a lover, he himself was in no position to criticise. People in glass houses...

Shirley bit her lip. Such thoughts were dangerous. What was past, was past. She thrust the letters at him.

'I don't know, Peter. These letters show, quite obviously, that Jeannette had a lover. They show that she stayed with him for part of the time when she left you. They show that the whole thing had more or less died when she returned to you.'

He shook his head.

'There's more to it than that,' he insisted stubbornly. 'Look at it like this. Jeannette meets this man – even invites him to a party at our house. Of that, incidentally, I'm pretty sure. The name is familiar, and I'm sure I've met him. However, an ... an affair develops, and a little later she leaves me and goes to live with him. She probably adopted an assumed name, and he set her up somewhere ... anyway, it's not important, the details, I mean. The fact is that eventually, he got tired of her.'

'Or she of him,' Shirley added quietly. 'She did come back to you, Peter.'

The set of his jaw distressed her; she didn't like to see him hurt.

'No. *He* tired of her. She came back to me only because it was the easiest thing to do. He gave her what she wanted – and she still wanted it. A fast life, a good time. When it wasn't available, she came back. That's all.'

He knew that Jeannette had not come back because she *wanted* to return to him.

'All right, you say he tired of her.'

'Yes. But though Jeannette came back home, she wasn't going to be put off so easily. She still wanted him. And I think she began to put pressure on him. The tone of that last dated letter tells us that. It tells us more. Let me read this to you – you must have skipped it–'

It was quite possible that she had. The first letter she had read with a curious detachment; its endearments had surprised, then shocked her in their intensity. The man with whom Jeannette had lived had not been averse to graphic descriptions of their affair, and of their feelings, physical and emotional.

The first two letters had made Shirley feel embarrassed, as though she were peering into other people's lives. The last letter she had read only cursorily.

'I won't deal with all of it,' said Peter. 'But just listen to this:

"'...darling, what you suggest is impossible. I must insist that it ends now. It was fun, we had a marvellous time, I took as much delight in your body as you did in mine, *but it is all now over*. I cannot see you again, I've no intention of taking up where we left off. As for the other suggestions you make, they're too damn' ludicrous, and I strongly advise you not to try them. I could always reply in kind of course, but I'm also aware that I've a damn' sight more to lose than you do. So I'm not going to reply in kind – I'm just going to give you a warning. Don't try it on. You do, and I'll break your sweet bloody neck. I've no intention of being hooked like this and I would much prefer that we should have pleasant memories of our encounters, than that it should all end by my being forced to do things to you that I should hate to do to any woman–"'

Peter stopped reading and looked up at her. His dark eyes were restless.

'You see what had happened?' he asked. 'He'd broken it off. She came back to me. But she still wanted him and she wrote to him, asking him to take her back. It's obvious that he refused, so she then told him that if their relationship was not to be continued she'd tell his wife about what had been going on. That's what he means about "having a damn' sight more to lose" – he's a rich man, but a lot of his backing is his wife's, and his reputation would suffer anyway if his sordid little affair became public knowledge.'

Shirley couldn't meet his eyes. She wondered if that was how Peter now looked upon the time that she and he had had together, during the months of Jeannette's absence. A sordid little affair.

'It never did become public knowledge. Jeannette must have written to him, or phoned him or something, to say that she intended to expose him in spite of his threats. So he stopped her talking.'

'That's going too far, Peter. You're introducing fancy in place of logic.'

'No, I'm not. Look, Shirley, it fits. Can't you see? He was desperate. Jeannette was pressing him. He came down – perhaps he was intending just to remonstrate with her, but when they met at the house perhaps Jeannette made him angry with her insistence.'

'Peter–'

'Perhaps he got violent and there was a struggle. He killed her. Then he realised that she might have some of his letters in her possession. He saw the desk, examined it, discovered the secret drawer and forced it. I suspect that he found a bundle of his letters and took them, overlooking these, which had fallen to the back of the desk. Then he left, fairly secure in thinking that there was nothing to connect them.'

Shirley took out a cigarette and lit it slowly. Pete's face was drained of colour. She regarded him calmly.

'Tell me,' she said quietly, 'do you *really* think that Jeannette was in love with this man?'

'I do,' he argued stubbornly.

'She was so in love with him that she was prepared to break up her marriage – and his? Even though he didn't want her?'

Peter looked at his hands, clenched on his knee. When he replied, his voice was strained.

'I think she was. I think it had become an overriding passion for her. Let me put you right on something, Shirley. After she returned, we didn't live together ... as man and wife. We had a difficult, strained relationship, an uneasy one. She often seemed preoccupied; she was out a great deal. I thought it was her natural reluctance, or inability, to settle immediately, after being away for so long. I realise now that I just didn't understand what was going on.'

He rose and walked across the room slowly, without looking at Shirley.

'We had lived together, she had been my

wife. But I didn't know her, I couldn't have known her. Or I'd have guessed what was going on. I didn't guess. I suppose it's impossible to know another person well enough...'

'You can't get inside another person's head,' said Shirley quietly.

'No,' Peter agreed. 'I realise that I didn't know what she was thinking about, or who she was thinking about. I should have recognised the signs, nevertheless. It doesn't matter anyway, not now. Perhaps it wouldn't have made any difference, even then. The fact is, Jeannette is dead.'

And looking at Peter, Shirley felt that perhaps a dead Jeannette presented a greater obstacle to Shirley Walker than she had done when alive. Angrily Shirley brushed the thought aside. Whatever had existed between her and Peter was over and done. And yet he had come to her now.

'Jeannette is dead,' he repeated slowly, 'and I know her murderer.'

'You can't say that,' Shirley insisted.

His face turned to hers.

'I think it merits looking into.'

'You mean you're going to tell the police?'

'No. I can guess what they'll say, in the first instance. First, not enough to go on. Secondly, I'm motivated by jealousy for my dead wife. I don't think they'd be right on either count. But even if they did act, they'd behave predictably. They'd interview him.

He'd cover up – he'll already have brushed over his tracks anyway, but the sort of warning that the police would provide would make a resourceful man like he is obliterate them entirely. He's already committed one murder–'

'Peter–'

'All right, I know, I can't say it. Maybe soon I'll be able to say it.'

'But if you don't go to the police?'

'Billy Sneed.'

'Who?'

Peter smiled faintly; it was the first time he had done so. It reminded her of other days, when he had smiled and laughed a great deal.

'Billy Sneed. You know the idea of the conventional private detective? Well, he's not it. Perhaps that's why he's so successful. He's so completely nondescript.'

'But how do you know him?' wondered Shirley.

'In divorce actions, the serving of writs, the tracing of relatives, he's an artist. I couldn't do without Billy Sneed. Nor could half the solicitors in the two counties. If there is anything on this man – if there are any marks unobliterated, Billy will find them.'

'I hope you know what you're doing, Peter.'

He shrugged.

'No. I don't know what I'm doing. All right, I agree it's really little more than the conventional shot in the dark. Jeannette had a lover. She is dead. He could be the killer. It's no more than that, for all my own conviction in the matter. So let's find out.'

'Why?'

'Why find out?' He regarded her carefully. 'You know why, Shirley. This man Crow, by visiting you, and then me, has shown pretty clearly that he thinks we're concerned in her death. We weren't. I want to convince him of it. And I can do it, this way.'

She couldn't meet his eyes.

'By pursuing the matter, you could discover more—'

'I know. More about Jeannette than I already know. But then,' he added desperately, 'I knew so bloody little, didn't I?'

That was the trouble, Shirley felt like crying out; you know so bloody little about me, too.

2

'Max Lavender.'

Billy Sneed chewed the name, rolled it round his tongue, swallowed it and sat there in digestive contemplation. Peter observed him for a little while as he hunched there in his dilapidated suit, his sad, thin face quiet, and his sandy hair thick at the nape of his neck, sparse at the temples.

'You know him?' queried Peter flatly.

'Of him. But then, Mr Marlin, it's my business to know of him. Though strictly speaking he's way out of what our American cousins would call my league. He's a bigger fish than what my clients would want to fry, in the usual run of things.'

Peter brushed one hand over his eyes.

'You've seen the letters.'

'Yes, and read them close, Mr Marlin. What is it then you want me to do?'

'You'll appreciate that this is all in strict confidence.'

'Mr Marlin, I'm surprised to hear you say that. I think you will agree that over the years of our association, and I may add that I done work for this firm before you were ever here too, you will have had no cause to suggest otherwise than that I have always been the very soul of discretion.'

The little man's tone was almost hurt, and his sad mouth drooped more than ever. He hitched at his jacket and did up an errant button, then went on,

'The very soul of discretion. You appreciate that in the delicacy of our relationship discretion is for ever necessary and you must know that you can count on me.'

'I'm sorry, Sneed. You're right, of course. It's just that – well, this is unlike the many other things you've done for me, and the firm.'

'I understand, Mr Marlin.'

And Billy Sneed did. Peter could sense the sympathy in his voice. This wasn't like the other things, because this was personal to Peter Marlin. He was involved in it.

'I quite understand, Mr Marlin. Most delicate, a most delicate matter.'

'What do you know of Max Lavender?'

Billy Sneed became businesslike, in a birdlike way.

'I know that he is a company director, and has some reputation in the City. I know that he's wealthy – though it is possible that he would not be able to put his hands on ready cash, if you know what I mean, Mr Marlin. Not ready cash of his own that is: his money will be tied up in his companies, but his wife is a wealthy woman in her own right – what the papers would call a minor heiress, I believe. She is somewhat older than him, though not so significantly that it could be said that he married her for her money.'

'Though it has been said.'

'Quite so. And there is possible truth in it. But in any case, with the backing of her money and influence, in the last twelve years he has built his own reputation in the City, and his stock is high. He knows some pretty important people.'

Peter chewed his lip thoughtfully.

'All this is pretty common knowledge, of course.'

'Of course, Mr Marlin. But I have had no previous occasion to delve any more deeply into Mr Max Lavender and his affairs.'

'But you think you could.'

'If you want me to.'

At Peter's nod, Sneed glanced down again at the letters in his hand.

'Is there any particular direction you wish my inquiries to proceed in?' he asked softly.

'The obvious one,' said Peter. 'Those letters show that Max Lavender had … had an affair with my wife. It's more than possible that she wasn't the first woman he knew outside his marriage, and more than possible that she wasn't the last. Indeed, I think that it may be that he threw her over for someone else anyway. I want you to find out. But more than that I want you to find out precisely what Max Lavender was doing on the night my wife died.'

Billy Sneed tapped a thoughtful fingernail against the letters, then carefully placed them on Peter's desk.

'You are of the opinion that Mr Lavender was involved in the death of your wife.'

'I think he killed her,' insisted Peter harshly.

'He might be able to show that he was elsewhere at the time of death,' commented Sneed mildly.

'He could still have arranged it.'

'And you wish to discover evidence of

such activity.'

Billy Sneed reached for his hat, which he had placed on the floor beside his chair. He rose, hesitating.

'Mr Marlin, I hope I am not presumptuous when I say that I think you should not bank too much upon my prospects of discovering what you want.'

'You think Lavender is unlikely to have killed my wife.'

'I didn't say that, sir. It's just that – the involvement may cloud your judgment and... I'm expressing this badly, but don't be too disappointed if nothing turns up.'

'He's an important man, Mr Sneed.'

'He is, Mr Marlin.'

At the door, Billy Sneed paused, a shabby figure in a nondescript raincoat. He looked back to Peter.

'It seems to me, Mr Marlin, that you finding the letters may be one thing. But is there anything else? I mean, you mentioned that the lock of the drawer had been forced. Where's the key? Have you looked for it? You might think that if she had hidden that key, there might be other things with it. Other things that might help.'

Sneed was right, of course. When Peter had found the letters he had thought of nothing else – other than ringing Shirley to tell her about the discovery. When he got back tonight he would have to make a thorough search of the house – and of the few things of Jeannette's that were still there. It would be distasteful. But it would have to be done.

Peter walked out into the office where Joan was at her desk.

'I'll be leaving early to-night, Joan. There are some things I've got to do at the house. So I want no calls this afternoon, all right? I've got enough to do in the office to keep me busy for the rest of the afternoon so I'm just not available.'

'Oh, Mr Marlin, yes, that'll be all right, but Mr Gaines just came in, a little while before Mr Sneed left. I told him you were busy but he said he wanted a quick word with you – and he's waiting outside.'

'Hell! Er ... all right, I'll see him, but not in the office. He might stay longer that way. I'll pop out to reception and have a word with him there.'

Sam grinned widely, and broke off the conversation he was having with the giggling Betty at the reception desk.

'Ah, the very man! Sorry to bother you, dear boy, but passing by, thought I'd pay my respects. And ask you whether you can fix the trustees' meeting for next Tuesday.'

'Hallo, Sam. Tuesday, Tuesday ... wait a minute.'

Peter stuck his head back around the door.

'Tuesday evening, Joan, isn't there something on?'

'Er … Mr John asked you to go to the Holford firm meeting, I gather.'

'Oh yes.' Peter returned to Sam. 'Sorry, Sam – you heard that, we'll have to fix another date.'

Sam Gaines smiled.

'Not to worry, Peter. Just that Mother wanted to have a dinner-party, and it would have been convenient to have the meeting afterwards. Can't be helped. Will you let me know as soon as you can make it? You couldn't come after the meeting, by the way?'

'No. Old Holford does tend to drivel on, and it's unlikely to be over before ten. Then there's a drive of an hour and a half and I'll need to stop off for a meal somewhere– I'd be too late for your mother and the others. But look, I'll get Joan to ring you and fix a date.'

Sam nodded slowly. He was suddenly serious.

'As soon as you can, Peter. I'd like to discuss the takeover, and the shareholdings of Amalgamated Industries in more detail, with you and Byrne. Right then, see you … and you be good, Betty, until I catch you one dark night, anyway.'

When Peter made his way back to his office the small knot of worry inside him was growing again. He sat in the leather arm-chair for what seemed an age, gnawing at his lower lip. Finally, impatiently, he

103

reached out to the intercom switch.

'Joan? Get me the Amalgamated Industries file. And put in a call for me. To Jackson. Mr Paul Jackson.'

3

Three days slipped past and there was no word from Sneed. The time passed uneventfully for Peter; the routine of the office remained routine. Stephen Sainsby was away in London and the strain that his presence would have imposed was avoided. Peter saw little of John either: he seemed preoccupied and was rarely in the office after lunch. Peter had spoken no more with him about his decision to go to the Bar. He wondered whether John had yet told Stephen, and doubted it. There would have been repercussions which would have reverberated around the office. Stephen was yet to discover that John was getting out.

Early on Monday afternoon Sneed telephoned Peter.

'Hallo, Mr Marlin. No, don't raise your hopes, I have little that is positive to report. I just ring you now to keep in touch, and to tell you that one of your hunches at least is correct.'

'How do you mean?'

'About Mr... I mean about a certain

gentleman's proclivities. He is, as you suspected, something of a womaniser. There is another lady at the moment in his favour.'

'I see. But what about his whereabouts on the night of–'

'Yes. On that particular night I fear that the gentleman has what is known in professional circles as an alibi. He would seem to have been playing cards – illegally, I believe – with a few male acquaintances of his in a little club off Jermyn Street. And yet...'

'Yes?' prompted Peter eagerly.

'Who knows? I must not rush fences. Possibilities abound, nevertheless. Fear not, Mr Marlin, that I am keeping your best interests at heart. I will be in touch again soon.'

'All right Sneed. As soon as you get anything, let me know.'

The call unsettled Peter. He prowled around the office. If only Sneed could root out something! If only he could show that Lavender's alibi was a false one! Playing cards with his friends ... friends could be bribed to keep their mouths shut when it was necessary.

Peter attempted to get some work done on the papers on his desk but was too restless. His mind was seething. Inspector Crow had not put in another appearance but Peter felt all the time that the man was there in the background somewhere, watching and

105

waiting. And Shirley hadn't been in touch with him – but why should she? She had already made things pretty plain. Events might have briefly thrown her and Peter together again, but she had no intention of being anything but coolly distant towards him. Perhaps it was as well. And yet ... there were times when...

He rose impatiently. Shirley and he – it was all over. She had shown she wanted it to stay that way. He strode to the door.

'Joan – any chance of getting Betty to make some coffee? Or get one of the juniors to do it, at least.'

Joan was on the telephone; she raised one hand, then covered the mouthpiece.

'Yes, I'll see to it, Mr Marlin. But there's a call coming through for you. Shall I put it through to your office?'

'Yes, all right,' said Peter absently.

As he went back in he heard her flick the switch. His phone rang, and he heard her door bang as she left the ante-room to seek out Betty.

He picked up the telephone.

'Mr Peter Marlin?'

The voice was quiet, and unfamiliar.

'Speaking.'

There was a short silence. Peter waited, puzzled. Then the voice came again.

'My name is Lavender.'

Instinctively, Peter glanced up to the door

– he wanted Joan to be able to listen in, be a witness to the conversation, but she had already left the ante-room. Excitement surged through him – excitement, and frustration at Joan's absence.

'What do you want?'

Lavender's reply came in smooth tones.

'No, Mr Marlin, it's I who should be asking you. What do *you* want?'

'I don't understand.'

'I think you do. I'm not a fool. It has come to my attention that for some reason best known to yourself you have begun to pry into my affairs. I want to know why.'

'You must be making a mistake, Mr Lavender. I–'

'I do wish you would not prevaricate.' The smooth tones had taken an edge. 'I'm an extremely busy man and you're wasting my time. I gather that questions are being asked about me by a certain disreputable little private detective who is favoured by the dubious name of Sneed. I don't like it, Mr Marlin, and I would ask you first to tell me what the hell you think you're doing, and secondly to persuade me that you will immediately cease this activity.'

'I have three letters in my possession, Mr Lavender.'

In the silence that followed, Peter could hear the man's controlled breathing.

'Letters?'

'Three. That you wrote to my wife. Two in affectionate, one in not so affectionate terms.'

Again there was a long pause. Then Lavender sighed.

'All right, so you know about Jeannette and me. It would be quite cynical, and pointless for me to say that I'm sorry. We don't know each other – though we did meet once, I believe – and let me assure you that … what there was between your wife and me, well, it didn't reflect upon you in any way, and in any case it's all over. I should say, it was all over before she came back to you.'

'But it wasn't all over for her.'

'What do you mean?'

'I think you know what I mean.'

'Listen, Marlin. I don't know what you're implying. I assure you that your wife and I – we finished it a long time ago. I've not seen her–'

'Think carefully before you say more, Lavender.'

'What the hell's the matter with you? Sore that you were cuckolded?'

Peter kept his temper with difficulty; the fact that Lavender was losing his helped him.

'My position in the matter is irrelevant. I'd just like to know more about yours. Such as where you were on the night that my wife died.'

Lavender's voice took on a harsh, brittle note.

'What the hell are you trying to say, Marlin?'

Peter was silent. The silence angered Lavender.

'Listen, Marlin, call off your blasted snooper. Do you hear me? I'm not having you or any filthy little detective creeping around prying into my affairs. Keep your nose out of my business, or I'll see to it that you never nose into anything again, ever.'

Lavender paused, and the malice in his voice became even more obvious.

'I can break you, Marlin, tear you into little ribbons. So stay away, do you understand? Stay away – or you'll pay for your snooping. Do you understand me? *You'll pay!*'

The receiver clattered. Quietly Peter replaced his. His calmness was a luxury, for euphoria surged through him.

Lavender had threatened him. So he must have something to hide.

Peter needed to get out of the office. He wanted to get some air. Wanted to think. Joan looked up in surprise as he walked out. She had a cup of coffee in her hand.

'Sorry, Joan. Changed my mind. You have it. I'm going out. Won't be back this afternoon.'

He walked down through the town till he came to the public park. The sun was warm and there were prams parked on the grass. Alongside the artificial lake there were wooden seats; Peter occupied the end of one and sat staring at the calm water.

Lavender was angry. Lavender was scared. He'd been rattled by the fact of Billy Sneed poking into his business.

So rattled that he'd found it necessary to telephone Peter, to remonstrate with him. Knowledge that Peter had the letters had made him even more worried. The next move must be Lavender's. It had to be. Peter could go to the police now – but if he waited, if he let Lavender simmer, if he kept the pressure on the man, who knew what would happen? Lavender could really take a false step. If the man had something to hide, as he obviously did, he could really take the plunge and betray himself. He'd gone some way along that path by phoning to-day. It all now depended on what Sneed could unearth.

For as yet, Peter himself had unearthed nothing in his search of the house. There remained only the attic bedroom. He'd be searching there to-night. And in his present frame of mind he would do better to make a start right now.

He drove home quickly. His euphoria had not deserted him. Things were beginning to move: it wasn't so much a question now of showing Inspector Crow that police suspicions about Peter and Shirley were unfounded; the excitement of feeling that he was near the truth behind the death of Jeannette now drove him on. It was almost with a feeling of relief that he swung into the driveway.

As he entered the house the telephone was ringing. It was the third important call he'd received that day: it was Shirley.

'Peter? I ... I just thought that I'd ring, to see if there'd been any further news.'

Her voice carried a note of doubt, as though she were not sure that he would believe her. It puzzled him.

'News in plenty. Sneed rang me this afternoon, to say that Lavender does have a current girl-friend – and then Lavender phoned.'

'Lavender!'

'The same. He didn't use the same words as he used to Jeannette, but the message was the same. If I didn't get off his back, I could look out for trouble.'

'He threatened you?'

'You could call it that.'

'I don't like it, Peter. Don't you think you ought to go to the police now? Particularly if he threatened you.'

'Don't worry, I'll go to the police – when I've got something more concrete. There's no record of the conversation, and we really need something more positive from Billy Sneed to pin Lavender down. No, there's time yet.'

'I think you should go to the police now, Peter. If Lavender threatened you–'

'You sound concerned.'

The silence that followed lengthened unbearably. It was Peter who broke it, lamely.

'Well, anyway, I'm hoping to find something – that key to the desk. Sneed thinks it might be here, perhaps hidden with other things. I've just got one room to check, but it's a hell of a job. She used to throw a lot of her old things in there, and there are cases...'

'Is there anything I can do to help?'

'You could give me a hand, here at the house.'

'I'm not sure that would be wise,' said Shirley slowly. The more decisively she added, 'But in the circumstances I think I will. I may be more likely to find it than you. You were always so damned untidy and unmethodical outside the office.'

She sounded almost like her old self.

And it was Shirley who found it – but not in the attic. She had gone down to make some coffee as the light faded in the attic and the dust swirled around them, making Peter sneeze. She suddenly called to him from the kitchen. The urgent note in her voice brought him downstairs immediately.

She turned to him as he entered the kitchen. She had donned an apron over her dark green sweater and slacks, and her face was flushed, her eyes excited. He had never seen her look so beautiful.

In her outstretched hand were two keys.

Peter took them from her quickly.

'This is the key to the drawer. But the other ... where did you find them?'

'In the sugar tin ... I ask you, in the sugar tin!'

Shirley was giggling with excitement.

'It must have been a temporary hiding-place for some reason,' mused Peter. 'Perhaps I'd come into the kitchen when she had the keys in her hand and she dropped them there rather than I should see them. Though why she wouldn't want me to see them – what is this key, anyway?'

It was short, thick and stubby. Deeply etched into the metal was a letter C and a number.

'C4976. Mean anything to you, Shirley?'

Before she could answer the doorbell rang.

'I'm not expecting anyone,' said Peter in surprise. He turned from the kitchen and went through to the front door.

It was Joan Shaw.

She was dressed in dark blue with a touch of white at her throat. Her red hair gleamed in the low sun setting beyond the trees. She was smiling a little nervously at him.

'Hallo, Mr Marlin. I thought I'd better call round–'

Her gaze slipped past him and he realised

that she had caught sight of Shirley, standing at the kitchen door, the apron at her waist, her face warm and excited. The smile on Joan's lips grew stiff at the edges.

'–to let – to let you know that the meeting at Holford's to-morrow night has been cancelled. I ... er ... I can't stop, I was just passing and thought that I could conveniently... I might not be in the office to-morrow...'

She turned abruptly and hurried away down the drive, almost running. He opened his mouth to call after her, but thought better of it. Slowly he closed the door, then turned to face Shirley. She wasn't looking at him.

'What on earth was all that in aid of?' he puzzled.

'She told you.'

'But she could have rung me – or left me a message at the office. Why shouldn't she be coming in to-morrow? And why did she run off like that?'

'I think,' commented Shirley slowly, 'that she was not expecting to see me here.'

'Yes, but–'

'And I think,' Shirley added, removing the apron, 'that I also should be going. Now.'

4

The interview room that had been set aside

for Inspector Crow was painted in a dirty cream, with dark green woodwork. They were serviceable colours perhaps, but hardly cheerful. It was possible that it was the depression induced by these surroundings that had taken the sharp edge off the attractiveness of the young woman who sat in the chair in front of the desk, and who turned now as Inspector Crow entered.

On the other hand, it could be the mere necessity of her visit that had dulled her, removed the vivacity from her face, the glow that he knew her hair could possess.

'Good afternoon, Miss Shaw.' He extended a bony hand to take hers. 'I do hope that I haven't kept you waiting.'

She shook her head, avoiding his eyes. It was curious how people – even those with nothing to hide – avoided meeting his gaze. When he was younger, and more conscious of and worried about his peculiar appearance, John Crow had thought that this failure to look at him had been due to an embarrassment induced by his skull-like features. Now he knew better: it was the fact that he was in the role of inquisitor, and whoever he was questioning – criminal, innocent, thug, parson, intellectual, moron – they all seemed to be unwilling to meet his gaze. It was as though they almost unconsciously felt that to reveal their eyes to him was to reveal their souls and while they might want to tell him something, there were always, always things they did not want to divulge.

In his experience the only ones who met his eyes confidently and honestly were the confidence tricksters; and with them it was all part of the stock in trade.

Crow dropped into the creaking chair that the local police had grudgingly provided for him. He drew a pad towards him, and looped his long fingers round the pen that he had earlier, carelessly, left lying on the desk. Martha always complained about his untidiness, but that was what good wives were for. How else could a man see his faults?

'Now, Miss Shaw, would you like some tea? No? well, I ask because the provision of refreshment is often relaxing in surroundings such as these. I apologise for them. They're dreary aren't they?'

'I suppose they are.'

Miss Shaw's nervousness was apparent; her unwillingness equally so. Yet she was here – and disinclined to indulge in small talk.

'You declared that you wished to speak with me,' Crow offered. 'I imagine that it will be in connection with the Marlin investigation.'

The red head nodded; her hands were hidden below the line of the desk, but Crow felt that they would be tight clenched, one inside the other.

'Yes. I have a statement to make.'

'You wish it to be taken down?'

'Yes.'

Crow nodded to the stocky young constable who stood just inside the door, his hands locked conventionally behind his back.

'Wilson will prepare a statement for your signature in a few minutes, but for the time being, just tell me about it.'

Joan Shaw was silent for a few moments. Then she raised her head. There was determination in the line of her soft mouth: she really was a most attractive woman, from which even the hardness in her eyes did not greatly detract. Many would not even see in her the possible lack of scruple which Crow seemed to detect; they would see only her beauty.

'You were at the office a few days ago,' she said slowly, 'and you spoke to me.'

Crow nodded gravely, and replied, 'You repeated to me the statement that you had already given to the police, concerning your whereabouts on the night of Mrs Marlin's death. I imagine now that you wish to retract that statement.'

'How did you—'

'Come, Miss Shaw, why else would you be here?' He regarded her sadly. 'What is it you want to tell me, Miss Shaw?'

117

For the moment she met his eyes.

'That I lied. That the statement was completely false. That I was not near the office that night.'

Inspector Crow lifted a hand to his mouth, absent-mindedly fingering the long dog-tooth. He stared passively at the girl, who had coloured slightly.

'Let me take this slowly. You were not at the office that night. It follows that you could not have seen Mr Marlin working there. We can assume that you had a reason for making the original statement, a reason which has now disappeared, or been overruled. This is perhaps of little consequence – in face of the knowledge that by making this new statement, which we'd assume to represent the truth, you are virtually telling me that Mr Marlin's assertion that he was in the office that evening must now remain uncorroborated.'

'I was not telling the truth earlier; I am telling the truth now.'

'Why?'

Joan Shaw looked puzzled; but it was an affected puzzlement. Crow was patient.

'Why change your story? We had accepted your earlier one – more or less.'

'I – I decided I couldn't keep on with the lie.'

'Even though the truth might injure Mr Marlin? After all, the original statement was made to protect him, wasn't it?'

She nodded, her eyes down to the floor.

'It was just that I felt I couldn't keep it up. Even for my – my employer's sake.'

Inspector Crow permitted himself an ironic smile. He wondered whether tears of contrition would soon emerge.

'Are you sure, Miss Shaw, that the first statement wasn't made to protect yourself as well as Marlin?' When her head shot up, he continued smoothly, 'After all, while your admission that you were not in the office means that Mr Marlin's presence there has not now been witnessed, it also means that we must now ask the question of you – if you were not there, where were you?'

'I–'

'And,' he added, 'why has no one denied that you were at the office? Perhaps your *own* actions that evening were unwitnessed.'

'I don't see why it is necessary to explain my own whereabouts that evening. Surely all I need to say now is that I lied earlier, to protect Mr Marlin.'

'You know better than that, Miss Shaw. I'm not going to ask why you should want to protect Mr Marlin–' as her colour rose, he added gravely, 'after all, any loyal employee would do the same. But you knew Mr Marlin and his wife, and both you and I realise that I must learn of your movements that night. Where were you?'

119

There was a long silence. Reluctantly, Joan Shaw finally admitted,

'Musgrave Hill.'

'That's ten miles away.'

'I went by car.'

'With?'

'At the office,' she said slowly, 'there's a man called Bill Daly.'

'Who will verify your statement?'

She shrugged, with an odd smile. It wasn't a pleasant one, decided Inspector Crow.

'Mr Daly,' he mused. 'I seem to recall that he's married, and this will be why he didn't come forward to deny that you could have been at the office that evening. I only wonder now why you yourself have changed your mind and come forward with the new statement.'

Her eyes did not meet his. She made no reply. He shrugged, and looked up at Constable Wilson.

'I think that the lady will make the statement now, if you'd like to sit here.'

He rose gauntly, and looked down at Joan Shaw. A pity about those eyes of hers; she really was an attractive woman. And knew it.

'I'll say good afternoon, Miss Shaw. I will, of course, obtain the necessary corroboration of your statement.'

He strode to the door in his usual ungainly fashion. For some reason he felt a little sad.

It would now be necessary to speak again with Mr Peter Marlin. But first a word with this man Daly.

And then there was this John Sainsby affair. It was curious how trouble moved in patches, like a slick of black oil on a calm sea. It could spread out and contaminate – and he had an odd feeling about Sainsby. His instincts told him that the man's problems would not be unconnected with the Marlin case, and yet there was no apparent reason to suppose so. There was no obvious link.

It was a pity. A pity about Marlin, and Sainsby. John Crow liked people. It unfitted him for police work. And yet he was still here after twenty years. Perhaps because although he liked people, he yet accepted that sometimes they had to be hurt, or injured, or demoralised – and that it was in the scheme of things that occasionally it was his hand that must bear the bludgeon.

5

'Of *entrecôte* steak,' Peter said, 'I was always inordinately fond.'

'I know.'

'This was a particularly fine specimen.'

'I didn't think it was a good idea, at first.'

'The steak?'

'You know what I mean. You coming here to-night.'

'And now?'

'I'm more inclined to accept that the idea was a sound one.'

'I'm pleased. But elaborate.'

Shirley leant back in the deep arm-chair and regarded him seriously as he sat casually draped along almost the length of the settee, one arm dropping to the carpet. He looked at home, and as though he had never been away from this house.

'I don't know whether elaboration is wise.'

'Try,' he urged.

'All right,' she said hesitantly, with a slight smile. 'I realise that you hope it will begin with a small apology at least, and I suppose it does. You see, I wasn't pleased when you came back here, the night after the coroner's verdict. I didn't want you here, because what there had been between us was over ... and I didn't want the complications that were likely to arise if you came back here. I was angry, and I said things that I perhaps didn't mean.'

'But which, nevertheless, carried the ring of truth.'

'Well, we'll say no more of that. The point was, I was a bit upset later when that inspector called because I felt it necessary to warn you – and that meant getting in touch and, well, you know what I mean, things could have got complicated.'

'I know what you mean. But they're not, are they?'

There was an odd note in his voice which she was unable to read. Doggedly, she plunged on with the words she didn't want to say.

'Then when I saw you again and you showed me the letters, and then again last night when I came over to your house, I realised that I was being tremendously adolescent about the whole thing. The past was behind us but there was no reason why we shouldn't be friends, knowing that complications aren't likely to arise because too much has happened to us to allow it.'

As there was no reason why she should now attempt to rationalise her problems out of existence like this. At least, no reason but one – and that was one she was unprepared to admit even to herself. She had already been hurt too much.

'I know what you mean.' Peter's dark head lay back against the arm of the settee. 'But the reason why I say I'm pleased is that when Jeannette came back I felt completely cut off from the world: I revolved around her, if you know what I mean. She always had that effect on me. It was why I never came back to see you and tell you – but let's forget that. The point is, that after she died I was *completely* alone, and I mean completely. The pressures were getting too much

123

– in a drunken way, I tried to say that to you when I came around the first evening...'

'Let's forget that, too.'

'Gladly. Anyway, when I found the letters I had to speak to someone, if only to marshal my own thoughts. You were the only person I felt I could speak to. And I've got to thank you again, too, for coming round last night.'

'You've already thanked me, by asking me to dinner.'

'Ah, but you refused, and we ended up here instead!'

Shirley laughed.

'It's only that I fancy my own cooking better than some of the rubbish they serve, and charge the earth for, in town.'

'There was always the country club.'

'I didn't really want to go there.'

Careful. There were pitfalls there. Peter used to go there with Jeannette; Shirley didn't want to go there with Peter; they'd be seen together, tongues would wag, the thought of an affair would come to their minds here in this room, problems, problems, careful, careful, careful.

Quickly, she said, 'Did Joan turn up at the office to-day, after all?'

Peter swung his legs down from the settee.

'I don't know exactly. I wasn't in this morning. She certainly wasn't there when I arrived this afternoon. Tell me, what exactly

124

was the matter last night? Why did she charge off like that?'

Shirley met his gaze calmly.

'Don't you know?'

'I wouldn't ask, if I did.'

'If you don't know, I can't tell you.'

'And you don't want me to pursue it. Women!'

'If you express such disgust in your voice again,' Shirley warned, 'I'll throw you out before ten.'

'Don't do that,' protested Peter. 'Particularly, since I've arranged for Sneed to call me here when he can this evening.'

'Oh?'

'Well, before 11.30 anyway.' He smiled. 'You see, he rang me this morning–'

'With news?'

'No, just to say that he hoped to have some more information by this evening. He sounded oddly ... well ... excited, you know. Anyway, he said he'd ring back, and I told him I'd be here and could be reached at this number till 11.30. I hope you don't mind.'

'Terribly. At least it means that I can legitimately present you with your coat at 11.31 without feeling that I have destroyed my image as a hostess.'

'You'd make a splendid hostess.'

'I'm not sure that remark was in the best of taste. I'll get some coffee.'

He sat there grinning as she busied herself

in the kitchen.

'Cigarette?' he yelled, after a while.

When she refused, he took out his cigarette case and lit one. Returning the lighter to his pocket he felt the key there and drew it out reflectively.

C4976.

What had Jeannette wanted with this key? Why was it sufficiently important to be hidden, impulsively it would seem, in a sugar tin? Why had she not retrieved it? What was it for? They were puzzling questions. Perhaps Sneed would be able to provide some of the answers when he rang, or when he returned.

Whatever they were, Lavender would be involved.

Lavender. Curiously enough, the anger that Peter had felt when he discovered the man's liaison with Jeannette had now dulled somewhat. It had become impersonal. The first sickening crunch that the knowledge of Jeannette's infidelity had brought had been eroded now, and this could only mean that his pride had exaggerated the importance of that discovery to himself. What he was really now admitting to himself, for perhaps the first time, was that his marriage to Jeannette had developed into an empty shell, a form that had lost its reality long before she had died. So personal feelings against Lavender had been violent in the first instance because he had *felt* that they should be violent: now their unimportance was recognised. Now, it was a question not of personal vengeance, but of making Lavender pay for the crime he had undoubtedly committed. He had been Jeannette's lover. And he had killed her.

'You've not discovered what that key is for yet?'

He was still holding it in his hand.

'No,' he said, slipping it back into his pocket to take the proffered coffee from Shirley. 'I think it's one of these public locker places – it seems too big and stumpy to apply to a household lock of any kind. But where or what the locker is I've no idea.'

'More important, what does it contain?'

Peter shrugged.

'More of friend Max's letters? Doesn't really matter. We've got enough on him now. I'm hoping Sneed will pick up more.'

Shirley glanced at the clock.

'He should be phoning soon.'

'And then you can throw me out.'

Sneed did not in fact telephone until 11.45. Peter was depressed, and on the point of leaving the house when Shirley's telephone rang. She ran to it, and then presented it to Peter.

'Mr Marlin? Sneed here.'

'Good, Sneed. I thought you weren't going to make it.'

'No. Later than expected.'

'Well, did you get what we wanted? Did

the information you expected reach you?'

The thin voice on the other end of the line was hesitant.

'Mr Marlin ... I think I'm right in saying that the alibi of the gentleman in question is somewhat less than watertight. I think it can be broken.'

'I knew it! I knew it could!'

'I'm afraid it's not quite that simple. I told you that the gentleman has a current girl-friend. It would seem that the alibi was concocted in order to disguise the fact that he was with her.'

'But *was* he with her?'

'This I have not yet been able to discover. I have spoken with her, but–'

'And even if she *says* he was with her is that necessarily conclusive? After all, one alibi can be broken, why can't a second?'

'Once again, Mr Marlin, this is something one cannot yet establish. However...'

'Yes?'

Again the odd hesitation.

'There is another piece of information, which I must bring to your attention con-cerning this matter, Mr Marlin – its – er – delicacy inhibits me from imparting it to you over the telephone. I am now on my way home. I think it would be best if I were to call in the morning–'

'Why not call in at my place to-night? Your taxi will be driving past.'

128

'Well … if you will still be up…'

'I'll be waiting.'

'In about an hour, then, Mr Marlin. At your house.'

Peter replaced the receiver.

'He's got some information about Lavender. He'll tell me at home, in about an hour's time.'

'You might as well wait here, Peter. I'll get you a drink.'

It was necessary. He felt tense and nervy. There had been an odd note in Sneed's voice and it had communicated an inexplicable nervousness. His stomach felt empty and his fingertips tingled. The sensation was an odd one, not excitement, not fear, but a mingling of the two. Shirley saw it, and tried to wean him away, to put his mind on other things.

'Have you seen Stephen Sainsby to-day?'

'He's in London.'

'What's happening about the partnership?'

Peter shrugged.

'I got the notice of dissolution a week ago now. In another two weeks I'll be on the way out. John has been working on the figures, I understand. I imagine that in a couple of days he'll have worked something out, and he and Stephen will present me with an offer of compensation for my share in the business.'

'What then?'

'I'll take it and get out, I suppose.'

'And then?'

'I've not really thought. Practise elsewhere, perhaps. Get a job with a commercial firm, go overseas, hell, I don't know. Is that all the time is?'

'I doubt if Sneed will be there before one o'clock... I think it's hard that they should throw you out of the firm like that.'

'They're probably right,' grunted Peter. 'I can see Stephen's point of view, if I think objectively. He'll get a shock just the same. John's leaving too.'

'Because of you?'

'Hell, no. As Stephen said, John's a man of principles so long as he doesn't have to stick to them. No, he's got reasons of his own. Something's worrying him – don't know what it is. Funny chap, John. So precise. So ... so careful.'

Shirley got up, with her glass in her hand. She seemed embarrassed.

'Yes,' she murmured. 'Peter, have you ever thought – have you ever wondered–'

'What?' he asked, surprised at her prevarication.

She was immediately confused, and laughed awkwardly.

'Oh, nothing, nothing... I was just being stupid.'

He thought no more of it. He had other preoccupations. He left Shirley at 12.50 and drove quickly down Gladstone Hill. The town was quiet. Tuesday nights died at 11.30 in this area. The traffic lights held him, and impatiently he thought of slipping through them. There were no other cars about. He held himself back. Shortly they changed.

It began to rain, lightly, as he left the other side of town, and his windscreen wipers left a smear, but not sufficiently impenetrable to make him stop and clean the windscreen. When he reached the house he hardly ran the car into the drive, but left it just inside the gate, its lights switched out as he came out of the street. He leapt out of the car and hurried for the front door. As he inserted his key he thought he saw a dim flash of light inside, and heard a light, clicking sound. Foolishly, he called out:

'Sneed?'

Foolish, because Sneed couldn't have got in, anyway. Unless he carried a skeleton key. And the only person who'd be likely to do that, thought Peter grimly, would be Inspector Crow.

He reached for the light switch just inside the hall door. When he depressed it, nothing happened. He swore. Light bulb, or fuse? He stepped gingerly through the darkness of the hall towards the kitchen. As he did so, his foot struck against something solid yet yielding at the bottom of the stairs.

Peter stood stock still. His pulse began to

race. Dimly, very dimly, he was able to make out a bulky shape on the floor. His foot pressed against it, warily.

At the same moment he heard a slight sound on the stairs at his back.

Instinctively he whirled, and out of the darkness of the stairs a white light stabbed at him, blinding him. He heard a rushing sound, the thudding of a foot and then something struck him heavily across the forehead. He was aware of the light as he fell backwards, slamming against the half-open front door, thundering it shut. Then the pain leapt at him again as another blow took him across the head and another. Feebly, he struck back, and felt a shoulder, against his hand, but consciousness was slipping away from him. The light faded in a whirling soundless time and then there was nothing…

Until there was the hardness of the door against the back of his neck, the throbbing pain in his head, the wetness on his face. There was the carpet under his fingers, something heavy – his hand, and leather, cloth, a hard, bony knee. Unwillingly, in the darkness, he leaned forward. His hand touched something cold. It was a face.

The hair at the temples was sparse. And matted with blood.

CHAPTER IV

1

It was the same appalling nightmare all over again – the nightmare that he had suffered when Jeannette had died. The police cars drawn up in the drive and the curious eyes in the road outside, the police, the photographers, the news reporters, but this time more numerous than before for now there was the added curiosity value: two people had died in this house.

And the nightmare was worse because of Peter's own physical condition. The doctor had attended to him immediately, in the house; his head was bandaged, but though the injuries seemed to be largely superficial they produced a throbbing headache of massive proportions. He had been taken to the hospital for quick X-rays but these had proved negative. There had been plenty of blood but no bone injury, no skull fracture.

By six in the morning he was propped up in a hospital bed, still half dazed. His fingers yet seemed to be aware of the hair and the blood: he couldn't get rid of the sensation. The door opened, and a man in a white coat stood framed in the opening.

'Good morning. How are you feeling?'

Peter grimaced, and the man came forward. He was tall, fair-haired, young.

'Head aching? Not surprising. No serious damage, though you've lost a little blood. Nothing that you can't make up.'

Peter squinted at him.

'We've met, haven't we?'

'Dr Cranmer. Yes. I knew your – we met at a party at your place one night.'

Peter closed his eyes. He remembered now. Cranmer … he had come to the house just the once, and he and Jeannette had spent rather a long time talking in one corner. That wasn't surprising: she had often talked to personable young men in corners. She liked to see the admiration in their eyes. Few of them managed to control it.

'I've seen your X-rays,' Cranmer was saying. 'Nothing to worry about. We'll keep you in here for observation till this afternoon, but you don't appear to be suffering from concussion either. I'm afraid your face will probably purple up though – around the eyes especially.'

He hesitated.

'The police will be in to see you shortly – about twenty minutes. Feel up to it?'

He sounded sympathetic. Perhaps it was because he had known Jeannette…

Half an hour later Inspector Crow entered,

134

in the company of a stocky constable. Crow took a seat beside the bed while the constable stationed himself just inside the door. The inspector's long legs stuck out at awkward angles and he looked distinctly uncomfortable. His face was sympathetic, but Peter had the feeling that the expression might not be sincere.

'Hallo, Marlin. How are you feeling?'

Peter grimaced. 'I could say all the better for seeing you, but I won't.'

Crow permitted himself a faint smile. It seemed to accentuate the narrowness of his jaw.

'You sound as though you may be on the way to recovery anyway. Now then–'

'Is he dead?'

Crow regarded him fixedly; the domed skull gleamed above his heavy eyebrows.

'I'm afraid Mr Sneed died almost immediately. The back of his skull was almost crushed. He had been beaten into insensibility. Why?'

'What do you mean, why?'

'He was killed, beaten to death with a brass paperweight. Just before I got here, I received the lab report – the brass carries only one set of fingerprints. They would seem to be yours.'

There was a long silence. Peter could hardly understand what Crow was trying to say.

'You must be crazy! Are you trying to make out that *I* killed Billy Sneed?'

'I'm not trying to make out anything, Marlin. At this time I am simply relating facts. Sneed is dead. In your house. The murder weapon carries your fingerprints – and no one else's. What comment do you have to make?'

Peter lay back and laughed. There was little amusement in it. Crow watched him with narrowed eyes.

'Well, Marlin?'

'It's beautifully fixed, isn't it? By God, I'll get that cunning–'

He stopped abruptly.

'I'd better tell you all I know.'

'That would be wise,' nodded the inspector.

Peter took a deep breath.

'I had an appointment to meet Sneed at my house–'

'You were employing him?'

'I was. To discover evidence that would fix the guilt of Jeannette's murder.'

'I see.' Inspector Crow cupped his narrow chin on his hands and leaned forward. His eyes were bright. 'You didn't tell me that you had any information that might lead to … the murderer.'

'You seemed to have an idea it was I. I knew I could prove otherwise when I found the letters. So I engaged Sneed to follow it up.'

'Unwise…' murmured Crow. 'But I am getting somewhat lost. Letters? What letters? I think you'd better start from the beginning.'

Peter did so. He told Crow of his feelings after their first meeting and of his discovery of the letters. Crow remained impassive when he learned the name of Jeannette's lover, but Peter detected a flash of interest in the man's eyes when he mentioned the threats that Lavender had made. He went on to relate the gist of Sneed's telephone call at Shirley's and his own visit to the house, to discover Sneed's body. He related the circumstances of the assault upon himself.

'Yes … the reason why the lights didn't work, it would seem, was that the main fuse-box had been damaged. Incidentally, the telephone lines had been cut also… You say that Sneed had some information to impart of a delicate nature. Any idea as to what it was about?'

'No. But it's easy enough to discover, isn't it?'

'Is it?'

'Of course. It concerns Lavender. All you have to do now is to arrest him, charge him with the murder of Jeannette and Billy Sneed and you'll soon sweat the whole thing out of him.'

'I'm afraid you've moving far too quickly for me,' said Crow quietly.

'But isn't it completely obvious? Lavender killed my wife. He thought that he had covered his tracks. Then he discovered that Sneed was investigating his whereabouts and got panicky. First he threatened me and got no change. Later the same day Sneed found his alibi could be broken, so what else could he do – particularly when it would seem that Sneed had discovered some other information, damaging to Lavender, that he was about to impart to me? He had to kill Sneed!'

'But at your house?'

Peter shrugged angrily. 'At my house – probably the opportunity didn't present itself earlier. He must have followed Sneed, saw him reach the empty house, and seized his chance. When I disturbed him he knocked me out too, stuck the weapon in my hand and beat a hasty retreat. Hell, it's all so perfectly obvious!'

'Not to me, I'm afraid, Mr Marlin.' Crow sighed. 'Did Sneed possess a key to the house?'

'No, but I don't see–'

'Then how did he get inside? I presume the house was locked?'

'Yes, it was, but it must have been Lavender who–'

'Lavender may have been your wife's lover, but do you really think he was in the habit of visiting your house? Would Mrs Marlin have given him a key?'

Peter saw the remoteness of the possibility: the affair between Jeannette and Lavender had been carried on well away from here.

'Perhaps I didn't lock the door,' he argued lamely. 'Perhaps they broke in.'

'They? Who? Sneed? Why should he break in? Lavender? How would he know that Sneed was going there?'

'I don't know!' Peter cried. 'You're the expert here. *You* tell me what happened!'

Crow shook his head sadly, irritatingly.

'I'm sorry, I can't do that, Mr Marlin. All I can do is to look at the provable facts and raise inferences from them in the absence of direct evidence from eye-witnesses. First item – there is no evidence that the house was broken into. Second item – Mr Sneed was killed by a weapon which bore your fingerprints. Third item – it would seem you had arranged to meet him there, assuming that Miss Walker corroborates that part of your story. Fourth item – all the lights were out. Why did you cut the wires, Mr Marlin?'

'I didn't cut the blasted wires!'

'A suspicious man might suggest that you did it and then left open the door to lie in wait as Sneed entered, expecting to meet you and eager to get in out of the rain. On the other hand you might have done it to make it appear that a prowler had entered and made sure that he wouldn't be disturbed by sudden lights.'

'That's nonsense! I didn't cut–'

'All right.' Crow suddenly became more brusque, dropping his sadly careful pose. 'Let's put some of your assumptions to the test. Let us suppose that your – er – assailant *had* a key and got to the house first, cut the wires, killed Sneed and then knocked you out and placed the weapon in your hand. That's what you want me to suppose, is it?'

'Yes.'

'Where was he when you entered the house?'

'Upstairs.'

'Why?'

'I don't know,' said Peter. 'I suppose he could easily have waited for me downstairs and hit me as I came in, instead of–'

'How did he know Sneed would come there?'

'I told you. He could have followed–'

'And got there first?' Crow pondered for a moment. 'Where were you the night your wife died, Mr Marlin?'

'Jeannette–? What the hell's that got to do with it?'

Crow's thin, lined face had saddened again.

'Miss Shaw paid me a visit yesterday afternoon. It would seem that she was not in the office that night. She did not see you there. There is no corroboration of your

140

story, therefore.'

Peter sat up, angry and puzzled.

'But why should she say this– I don't understand–'

Crow's voice was slow and measured.

'It would seem that she has been – ah – involved with Mr Daly at your office.'

Peter remembered fleetingly the looks on the faces of Joan and Daly when he entered the office the other day.

'But he's married!'

'Precisely. On the night in question she was with Mr Daly. There are obvious reasons why he did not come forward to say that Miss Shaw was not telling the truth when she said she had seen you at the office that night. He knew she couldn't have seen you – but he could not say so for fear of exposing himself to the risk of his wife discovering his infidelity.'

'I still don't understand why Joan–'

'In spite of her playing around with Daly,' commented Crow smoothly, 'it would seem she yet nursed a certain – ah – affection for you. I would imagine that she felt she was helping you. It is just possible that she thought that you might have killed your wife. Perhaps she then assumed that after it had all blown over, with your wife dead, you and she might–'

'Yes,' said Peter slowly. 'Yes, that day in the office…'

'Something then happened to make her realise that her daydreams were just that – nothing more than daydreams and she realised that you and she were never going to – well, something happened to make her wish to tell the truth. She came to me yesterday.'

'She'd been to my house the previous night,' said Peter harshly. 'She saw Shirley Walker there.'

'Ah ... and realised,' mused Crow, 'that she would never be more than third best, if that– I'm sorry, Mr Marlin. I should not have said that.'

Peter shrugged. He had other things to worry about than the implications of that remark.

Crow stood up and clasped his thin hands behind his back; it had the effect of making him stoop slightly and when he walked across to the window and stood staring out, with his back to the room, Peter had the fanciful thought that the man looked like some hunched, evil bird of prey, with his great skull gleaming in the grey morning light.

'This is rather an unusual position in which I find myself,' murmured Crow. 'You are a solicitor; yours is not a criminal practice, but you are aware of the mechanics as well as I. You need make no statement to me, of course, and this you well know. But I would strongly suggest that you engage a solicitor for yourself – don't try to handle the matter on your own. One's objectivity is difficult to maintain when one is personally involved … facts get twisted, ideas, theories remain unformed.'

'Are you trying to say that you're thinking of charging me?'

Crow didn't turn round. His hands were quiet.

'Look at the situation as it stands, Mr Marlin. *You* say you were at the office when your wife died. That is now unsubstantiated. You discovered her body. What motive could you have had for killing her? She had taken a lover. You had discovered this, and killed her. You think yourself relatively safe, but the pressure builds up and so you "rediscover" the letters, which you had in fact found some time before, engage Sneed, frighten Lavender, then stage this situation last night…'

'In the meanwhile bashing myself over the head.'

Crow looked back at him, seriously.

'There are holes, obviously, but the general thesis sounds rather convincing – particularly when you would seem to have re-engaged the attentions of Miss Walker. You will appreciate that I am being very frank.'

'Very.'

'Your injuries, of course, could have been unforeseen by you in the planning stage – perhaps they were caused in the struggle with

Sneed. You could conceivably then have deliberately knocked yourself out against the door – there is some of your blood there.'

'And my motive?'

'To place the guilt for the death of your wife on another – and to be free to move on … to other fields.'

Peter's lip curled at Crow's delicacy. 'I'm surprised you haven't charged me already!' he snapped.

Crow smiled again, turning from the window. 'I'm an experienced police officer. I don't jump before I'm pushed. If I don't have a strong enough case you know more than enough law to have *me* in the dock, and I have no doubt that your professional colleagues would be quick to lend a hand. No, it seems to me that–'

'The key,' said Peter flatly.

'I beg your pardon.'

'The key. In my jacket pocket, look quickly!'

Crow wasted no time in arguing. He moved to the wardrobe, took out Peter's jacket, and went through the pockets.

'This it?'

'No, that's the key to Jeannette's desk. There should be another there.'

'There isn't.' Crow stared at the key lying in his hand.

Peter lay back, thinking furiously. Crow watched him narrowly for a moment, then came across to the bed.

'What about this missing key?'

'I found it – or rather, Shirley did. In the sugar tin. It must be why Lavender was in the house *before* Sneed. He was looking for that key!'

'You will forgive me, but I am particularly obtuse this morning.'

'Don't you see? When Lavender killed Jeannette he found some of his letters to her and took them, having forced open the drawer of her desk to do so. They didn't comprise *all* the letters, but they were all he could find. When he learned that I had *three,* he knew there must be others still in the house so he had to come back again, to look for them. *That* was why he broke in ... all right, *got* in somehow, searching for the letters. Or even the key itself. Perhaps he knew she'd keep them in a deposit box. But Sneed arrived, and Lavender killed him. Then I came. That was why he was upstairs ... he was still looking. He didn't know I'd already got the key. So after he attacked me he thought he'd plant Sneed's murder on me. He went through my pockets, found the key, and knew he had everything going smoothly at last.'

Peter took a deep triumphant breath.

'He could have Jeannette's murder pinned on me, and Sneed's, and he had his letters back.'

Crow regarded him thoughtfully. Some of

Peter's exuberance died.

'For a lawyer,' commented Crow, 'you are singularly unpreoccupied with detail. I repeat, there was no sign of a break-in. Moreover, if *you* had three letters in your possession, what was the point of searching for the others? Wouldn't the three, in your thesis, be enough to damn him? And in any case, you're wrong about Mr Lavender.'

'What do you mean?'

'We already knew,' said Crow tiredly, 'from our earlier inquiries, all about his affair with your wife, about his alibi, about the fact that on the night Mrs Marlin died he was really with ... another lady, not his wife, who can testify to that effect–'

'And you'd believe her?'

'We have to believe somebody,' said Crow mildly. 'The point is, he had nothing to gain in breaking in, or letting himself in with a key or what have you. Even so...'

'You can check on the key. I had it when I left Shirley.'

'That's easy to confirm. She's outside now.'

'Shirley–'

'What was the number of the key? Describe its appearance.'

Peter did so. Crow turned to the constable.

'Wilson, get it checked. I want to know if it is a deposit box.'

The constable left. Peter was staring at

Crow with cold eyes.

'You're convinced of Lavender's innocence.'

Crow spread his bony hands. 'The evidence—'

'He's a wealthy man. Influential.'

Crow looked at him thoughtfully. 'He can account for his movements on the night of your wife's death.'

'Who got on your back, Inspector Crow, and told you to call the bloodhounds off Lavender?'

Inspector Crow stood still. His thin form seemed to impart more menace than ever; his long fingers were slightly crooked as they hung at his sides. But his voice was surprisingly mild in tone.

'Arrogance seems out of character in your make-up, Mr Marlin. Would you like to see Miss Walker now?'

2

As they drove in the police car to the railway station Crow was angry. It was not often that he permitted himself that luxury. Over the years he had come to accept that his feelings were wont to intrude upon, and perhaps to some extent affect, the efficiency of his work, but he made their effect minimal. They were, after all, simply problems that arose from sadness he sometimes felt for the foibles of human nature, or from the genuine respect or liking that he occasionally felt for people with whom he had to deal. So many of the individuals who crossed his path were criminal, but not in the basic sense: momentary aberration, weakness, background, intense provocation, these could all destroy a man who was inherently decent, and cause him to commit a criminal act. Crow knew this and had come to accept the feelings that sometimes arose in him when he was faced by such people.

But anger was another matter entirely.

Anger was something he could not afford. The other, unprofessional emotions did not impinge upon his duty too much: he could compensate for them, react against them. They did not affect his judgment, his clarity of thought. But anger was different: it muddied his brain, it was a slow mist that crept across his intellect, it thrust excitement into his veins when he needed to remain cool.

And he was angry now.

It had been wrong of Gray to telephone him. It had been wrong of Gray to put him in a completely false position. Gray had been using his own position, and the fact of his own friendship, to interfere in matters that were exclusively Crow's problems. This was a murder investigation. Gray shouldn't have phoned. He had, of course, prepared the ground well. He'd begun by discounting his rank, and had continued, talking in friendly vein, about the old days when they had worked together.

'By the way, John,' he had said off-handedly, 'I gather you've set the local boys on to Max Lavender.'

'That's right. We've managed to pick up a lead that tells us that the murdered woman spent some months in his company.'

'You're always so damned puritanically cagey, John. You mean Max Lavender had been sleeping with her, had a flat set up for her in town.'

'If you like. Anyway, it's worth following through. I heard that the story he gave us as to his whereabouts might well be false.'

'It was.' Bill Gray's voice had been cool. 'I've got the reports in front of me, John. He was in fact with one Sally Baxter, his latest light-o'-love. I've interviewed her myself. That's where he was. So he's not implicated in this Marlin woman's death.'

'But–'

'John, take my word for it.' Gray's voice had hardened. 'I'll send the stuff on down to you now, so you can see for yourself. The fact is, there's no point in pursuing inquiries in that direction.'

'You're telling me to stay away from Lavender?'

'You could put it like that,' Gray had replied suavely. 'Need I spell it out for you? He's not involved. You have my word.'

'And–?'

'All right, and the word is that he's been bothered enough. I presume you get the message, loud and clear.'

Crystal clear. Crow bit his lip; the car sped through morning streets, but he saw nothing. Lavender had been cleared on a woman's word, and the matter was to end there. Why? Because, as Marlin had said a few hours ago, Lavender was a wealthy and influential man. He moved in exalted City circles; rumour could damage his reputation, and stains of that nature affected many people in high places, people who had investments to think of, financial deals fluttering in the wind. Lavender had picked up a telephone and complained – and he'd got results. At the end of a few more, lesser lines, had been Commander Bill Gray.

And John Crow had done as he was told.

Lavender must have been as mad as hell when he discovered that Marlin had engaged Billy Sneed to make further inquiries. Certainly mad enough to warn Marlin off personally. But mad enough to kill?

In the car mirror Crow could see the white swathed head of Peter Marlin. The man had said nothing during the long drive. The girl – Shirley Walker – had also remained quiet. Why had he allowed her to come along? One never knew about such things: his cold official explanation, the one he admitted to himself, was that it gave him an opportunity to observe them closely in each other's company, to seek out the nuances, the inferences that might be obtained from a glance, a word, a movement when they were together. On the other hand it could be that it was because he felt that she had a right to be there, as Marlin did, when they reached the railway station. But Crow was conscious that there could be other, more human reasons, for his allowing them to come.

These he was not going to admit to himself, nor dwell upon them. It was enough for him to know that his weaknesses were his weaknesses.

They swung at last into the broad approach to the station. It was two hours since Wilson had returned with the confirmation that the number of the key tallied with that of a deposit box at Cardington railway station. It would be one of a series of lockers, paid for on a time basis. They had waited only for Marlin to get dressed before they had left in the police car.

Marlin seemed none the worse for the drive, though he remained a little pale. The hospital hadn't made a great fuss about his release.

The station master was waiting for them, pompously, at the station entrance.

'Inspector Crow? Glad to meet you, sir. The lockers are this way.'

He moved ahead of them chattering, a short, plump man in a regulation uniform that did nothing for his figure. Crow cut into his chatter.

'Has no one been near the lockers yet? The one in question hasn't been opened?'

'No indeed, sir. I've had a man on duty there all morning, sir. No. C4976 I think you said it was. It will be just along here and Fred will be–'

The long row of lockers faced them blankly, grey boxes lined six high, one line against the wall, another double line forming a narrow corridor. The station master was looking round into the corridor.

'Fred! Fred Davis!'

'Blast!'

Crow pushed himself past the waddling station master with an angry exclamation. He moved quickly down the row of lockers. Then he stopped.

The locker he stared at was number C4976. The key was in the lock.

He felt Peter Marlin thrust an arm past him to drag open the locker door. There was nothing inside.

'Fred Davis!' The station master's voice echoed shrilly around the booking-hall.

Crow looked at him coldly. 'We'll go to your office, if you don't mind,' he said quietly. 'Wilson, I'll want that key dusted for fingerprints. There won't be any, but we'll have to check.'

'What the hell has happened?' Peter Marlin blazed. Justifiably, in Crow's eyes. Crow shrugged, and led the way to the station master's office. The pompous little man was crushed.

'Really, Inspector Crow, I don't know what to say. I – Fred! There you are at last! What on earth–'

Fred was youthful, pimply, and un-abashed.

'Look here, I been standing there all mornin' just starin' at them lockers and no one didn't think of bringin' me a cup of tea, did they? There I was, with me tongue hangin' out by ten and no one–'

'You left the lockers at ten o'clock?' asked Crow quietly.

Fred's eyes grew round as he took in the sight of Inspector Crow.

'Cor ... you ... yes, well, about ten-fifteen. I just went for a cup of tea and–'

'It's now eleven o'clock,' snapped Marlin, standing just behind Crow.

'Well,' countered Fred with a defiant lurch of his shoulder, 'you got to let it have time to go down, don' yer?'

'You saw no one approach that locker?'

'Well, no, not while I was there, but–'

'You couldn't see it from the tea-trolley?'

'Well, there's a kind of sign which sort of juts out an'–'

'You couldn't see.'

'No. That's right.'

'Fred Davis–'

The station master was rising menacingly. Crow silenced him.

'Thank you, Mr Davis.' Fred left, still defiant. 'That's *your* staff problem,' Crow continued addressing the station master, 'From our point of view it's too late now. What information can you give me about that locker?'

'I've got it here,' gasped an empurpled station master. 'We have an arrangement whereby we allow individuals to lease a locker over a period of time, if they wish. They retain the key, and pay when they return it. It's on a monthly or three-monthly basis.'

'This locker?'

'It was leased for a month, ten months ago, and then re-leased, by post, quarterly. To a Mrs Jean Matthews.'

'Or Jeannette Marlin,' said Peter harshly.

'Was it continually used?'

'Oh, that we can't say. If the key is out, that's it. We don't inquire–'

'I see,' cut in Crow brusquely. 'Is there any other information you can give us about it?'

'I'm afraid not. You see, I–'

'Thank you, we'll take no more of your time.'

Crow stepped out of the office. He walked slowly across the booking-hall, the others following just behind. He stood staring at the lockers. Pity. At some time between ten-fifteen and ten-fifty-five someone had opened that locker with the key that Peter Marlin claimed was in his pocket last night. It didn't mean, of course, that Marlin couldn't have arranged for someone else to open that locker and remove the contents...

In the background the station master was hovering anxiously. But Crow paid him no attention: Marlin and the girl had moved behind him out of his line of vision. They were standing just beyond the end locker to Crow's left, and Shirley Walker was saying something in a low voice.

'Did ... did you see that man, as we came into the booking-hall?'

Peter's reply was inaudible.

'But he looked as though he knew you,' came the girl's insistent voice. 'And he looked away, as though he didn't want to be recognised. *Do* you know him?'

In the short pause that followed Crow moved quickly, close enough to catch the reluctant reply.

'Yes ... I know him ... slightly. He's called Jackson.'

They were moving away from the lockers now.

'Paul Jackson...'

CHAPTER V

1

When Peter entered the office on Thursday morning Betty was so surprised that she actually left her seat and intercepted him.

'Ooh, Mr Marlin, are you all right? I heard that–'

'Yes, thank you, Betty. I'm quite all right.'

He couldn't prevent the smile that came to his face at the sight of Betty's eyes, riveted to the discolouration around his temple and eyebrow.

'You really got a bashin', didn't you, Mr Marlin!'

'Yes,' replied Peter gravely, 'I really got a bashing.'

He went on up the stairs. Joan wasn't in the ante-room, but he wasn't surprised. It was a difficult situation. She would obviously wish to see as little of him as possible, but would she leave the firm now? He hoped not; he had no quarrel with her for telling the truth, even if she had been moved to do so by the belief that he had taken up with Shirley again.

Had he?

He opened the door to his office. It remained to be seen; he wasn't sure of his own feelings yet, let alone hers. He also had to admit to himself that the realisation that he had known so little of what Jeannette was thinking about, what she *was*, tended to make him reluctant to enter another emotional entanglement. He smiled wryly. Assuming that one could avoid an entanglement. He suspected that such things happened with little control of the situation being possible.

But he really must try to get in touch with Joan, persuade her to come into the office, carry on with her job. It wouldn't be long now before he would be leaving Martin, Sainsby and Sons and it was foolish that she should relinquish her job in the circumstances.

He rang reception. Betty answered at once.

'Betty – I gather Joan isn't in to-day. Can you ask one of the juniors to call up here in about an hour's time to do some filing for me. I've a stack of stuff to deal with. Oh, and Betty – do you know if there have been any calls for me? No? Well, if there are later, put them straight through to me here.'

He opened the appointment book. Three only, all of which he could push off on to Daly or one of the other experienced legal executives. And lunch with the Round Table. Better give that a miss: there might be a certain amount of strain. There might even be a certain surprise to see him there out of Crow's clutches.

Peter himself had been a little surprised at Crow's attitude. They had returned to the police-station and Peter had made a written statement. Crow had paced around the room on his long, thin legs and then sent the amanuensis out. He'd turned to Peter and Shirley then and said,

'I've decided to press no charges at this stage. I'll be perfectly frank with you, Mr Marlin. I'm not happy at your involvement in these two murders: a great deal remains to be explained. But while I yet harbour certain suspicions, you will know as well as I that the case I have is entirely circum-stantial – and while circumstances have hanged men before now, in this case there are too many doubts.'

He had resumed his pacing.

'You will shortly be leaving your firm,' he had continued. 'I would be happy if you saw fit not to leave the area – or at least, if you kept closely in touch with the police if you wish to leave. I'm doing nothing so melo-dramatic as to place you under surveillance, but I think you will appreciate that so far as I'm concerned you are certainly not out of the wood. Miss Walker agrees with you that you held the key to the locker before you left her; you say that the key was stolen from you. I yet need to know why it was stolen, why it was important, and who could have stolen it. We will now be pursuing various lines of investigation ... to which our inquiries concerning you will be peripheral.'

He smiled suddenly, though not warmly.

'In other words, you can go – for the time being. And if anything else of relevance occurs to you, which might assist in our investigations, I'd appreciate your getting in touch with me – rather than going off at half-cock on your own.'

He didn't add that Peter's actions had already cost one life but the unspoken words were there between them.

Peter sighed and riffled through the papers on his desk. He still hadn't dealt with Mrs Davies's matrimonial problems. Perhaps it would be better if he handed the whole thing over to John Sainsby. He read quickly through the few letters that had arrived yesterday, but found himself unable to concentrate. Inspector Crow's last words, as Peter left, kept returning to him.

'And Mr Marlin ... I think that Mr Lavender has become an obsession with you, or is in danger of becoming so. You are making a mistake.'

Was he making a mistake? Was the possibility of Lavender's implication in Jeannette's death becoming obsessional?

It had all seemed so obvious, so logical. Who else would want to kill Jeannette? Who else would have reason, or motive, or desire? Why was she killed? Who could possibly—

Peter suddenly felt cold. There was always the possibility that Lavender had not been Jeannette's only lover. There could have been others. He shuddered: he was just beginning to realise how completely he had been unaware of the reality behind Jeannette. She had been his wife. They had lived together. But he did not know her. He had never known her. She had been bright, vivacious, lovely, exciting – and to his knowledge she had taken a lover. One lover. But what else didn't he know about her?

The tap on the door made Peter start.

Surprisingly, it was Stephen Sainsby.

'Hallo, Peter. Busy? Mind if I come in for a moment?'

He walked slowly into the room, one hand in his trouser pocket, the other dangling at his side, as usual displaying the regulation inch of shirt-cuff, white, unsullied. His aristocratic features were smooth and unworried, but Peter sensed an unease about the senior partner that was uncharacteristic.

'Mind if I sit down?'

At Peter's nod he dropped into the armchair facing the desk. In doing so he took his hand out of his pocket. The knuckles were bandaged. Peter stared at the hand.

'It seems we've both been in the wars,' he said slowly.

'Hah – yes. Barked my knuckles on the edge of the electric hedge-trimmer. Damned lethal thing! And you, my boy, how are you feeling?'

'Somewhat conspicuous,' remarked Peter dryly, touching his eye.

'It's as well you can smile about it,' said Stephen, stretching his legs out in front of him and staring at his shoes. They were narrow and fashionable; dark grey suède. He was silent for a moment.

'Got a man upstairs,' he grunted. 'I'd like you to see him. Unpleasant matter. Blackmail. Never could take to such matters – largely because I always felt that if these damned people had behaved themselves in the first place they wouldn't now be in the fix they are.'

'You're particularly moral this morning.'

'Am I? I don't know. It just seems to me that there are things one can do and things one can't. A decent life. It doesn't take a great deal to behave in a responsible manner. But people are foolish, and weak, and amoral – and then they run weeping to us, and often there's not a damn' thing we can do about it. Except write a silly little letter, or call in the police. People these days – I must be getting old.'

'I'll see him in a few minutes,' said Peter quietly.

Stephen Sainsby's lean fingers fiddled

absently with the immaculately knotted tie as his grey eyes held Peter's.

'Good,' he said suddenly. 'But that's not the only reason why I came in. I had a couple of things to say. First, I'm glad to see you back here – I heard about the attack upon you, and I was coming around to the station when they told me you were being released. Anyway, I'm glad you're all right. Second, I think that I must apologise.'

Peter's eyebrows lifted. Sainsby bared his teeth in a bright caricature of a smile.

'You look surprised. But even I can apologise. I got angry, the other day. We had a – set-to in my office. I shouldn't have lost my temper. We should have settled the whole thing more amicably. I am sorry. I would wish that we would part on more friendly terms.'

He sounded sincere. Peter felt slightly shamefaced. He shrugged.

'I don't really think that your apology is necessary, Stephen. I know how you felt. You were right, of course. My staying on could do the firm nothing but harm. It was I who should have offered to get out. I can only plead that your request was a shock–'

'I know, my boy, I know. It's just that I was always certain that you would put the firm first, and that you would do the right thing, and then when you were a bit ... er ... difficult, I lost my temper. Anyway, all over now, eh?'

Pat me on the head and call me a good boy, perhaps give me a sticky piece of chewing-gum, thought Peter sourly.

'That's right, Stephen,' he commented.

'Good,' said Stephen briskly, rising athletically to his feet. 'Now, two other things about your leaving. First, young Jenkins has been with us as an articled clerk and his results will be out next week. Do you think we should take him on as an assistant?'

'He's a good lad. You should take him on, with the offer of a junior partnership within two years.'

'Yes. Good. I think he would fit in well. Now, the other matter. I've gone over John's figures – he let me have them yesterday. I think he's been a bit ... er ... generous in his estimates, but I'm not inclined to quibble about it. He suggests that a fair share in the assets, which you would take out with you, would be two to two and a half thousand. What's your reaction?'

Peter thought of the long nights in this room; the nights when Jeannette had been in Lavender's bed.

'I'm not going to argue over that figure,' he said.

'Fine! That's settled then! Somewhere between those two figures, work out the details with you end of the week.'

The smile on his lean face was genuine

now. He probably knew damned well that he was getting his partner out of the firm cheaply. Peter had no doubt that John's figures would have been around the three thousand mark. To hell with it all!

'Good. Well, I'll send down this chap from upstairs.'

Stephen Sainsby sauntered to the door. His uneasiness had evaporated. He obviously thought that he had managed things very well: both his apology, which was the softening-up process, and the agreement over the partnership share, which was the kidney punch. And yet there was something else too, an excitement that communicated itself to Peter, a satisfaction present in the man's bearing.

The reason came when he finally reached the door. Stephen paused there as though remembering something. When he looked back, his thin, handsome face was impassive but there was a glint of triumph in his eyes.

'By the way,' he said casually enough, 'I had dinner with Lord Leyton last night. I ... er ... I was led to expect that before long we're likely to see an announcement in the newspapers. Nothing official yet, of course, but it looks as though I'm going to be ... er ... elevated, as they say.'

'My congratulations,' Peter said dryly.

When the door closed quietly behind the senior partner Peter grimaced. The old man had done it at last. His socialising, his good works, his elegance, his political speech-making, his good, solid, solicitor background had enabled him to pull it off.

A title among the principals of the firm would look fine on the headed notepaper. Stephen Sainsby, C.B.E. – or perhaps even Sir Stephen Sainsby. But whose name would appear below it? Not Peter's – nor, it would seem, John Sainsby's. Unless he changed his mind.

One thing was certain. John hadn't told Stephen yet.

2

The man who sat in front of Peter was known to him in a vague fashion: his was a face that was familiar. They had certainly not moved in the same circle, but Peter had seen this round, chubby, good-natured face in the country club and at a few other functions besides. His name was Mr Prudhoe, and he owned a small chain of retail draper shops in the two counties. He was perhaps more than moderately successful in the business world, and as far as Peter knew, Prudhoe was respected as a cheerful companion, a man who could hold his liquor even if he did get rather boisterous in his cups, and one who retained a sense of business in spite of his more flamboyant gestures.

But it would seem that he had made one flamboyant gesture too many. It was with considerable reluctance that he told Peter; he left the impression that he would have preferred to deal with the older man upstairs. It was a common enough story. His wife was an invalid, and bedridden. She was unable to accompany him on his social outings—

'—which I undertake, mainly for business reasons, you understand, Mr Marlin—'

He thought a great deal of her, but inevitably there were occasions when a young woman swam into his vision and made him think of other things than business. One such young woman was Susan Varley.

Peter knew her too, in an equally vague way. She was about twenty-five: old enough to know what life was all about. She had hovered on the fringe of Jeannette's evenings at the country club at one time. However, it would seem that she had caught the eye of Mr Prudhoe.

'You know how it is, I danced with her, and thought she was, well, a bit of a dish, if you know what I mean, a nice bit of crackling, but that was that.'

For the first time. But Mr Prudhoe had seen her again, on a less formal, less crowded occasion, and Susan had made it quite obvious that while she would not be prepared to regard him in a serious light, she would certainly not be averse to casual encounters in lonely places, provided the price was right.

'Now don't get me wrong, Mr Marlin. I mean, she's not the kind of girl to demand money, but you know, there are other ways in which a chap can show his appreciation for an understanding girl...'

And Susan had certainly completed his education in that direction. There had been a couple of trips to London, and shopping sprees on those occasions had considerably lightened his pocket.

'Mind you, I'm not saying she wasn't worth it. No, indeed.'

He spared Peter the details but left no doubt in his mind that Susan's perform-ances were more than up to scratch.

'And then, Mr Prudhoe?'

'And then I got this letter.'

It would seem that things had got rather difficult at home and Prudhoe had found it virtually impossible to get away for his occasional encounters. With considerable expressed regret to Susan, and just a little unexpressed relief to himself, he had called a halt, and Susan had accepted the kiss and good-bye without rancour. It had been the basis of their arrangement all along. No ties, no problems. But then, a month after it was all finished, the letter arrived, posted locally, white paper, white envelopes, carefully typed.

Peter read it. It contained nothing startling. Its statements were short, and bold.

'Dear Mr Prudhoe,

I have kept a very close watch on your movements. You've been sleeping with Susan Varley. Your wife is ill. Were she to be informed of your conduct what would happen? You can buy my silence – for £500. Used notes. Not consecutive numbers. Ring Musgrave 291 at 8 on the 29th. Matters will proceed from there. And remember. Tell the police, and the news of your conduct will be all round town. After it reaches your wife.'

It was unsigned.

'I rang the number,' said Mr Prudhoe. 'It was a public call-box. There was no reply.' He appeared shamefaced.

'No further letter?'

'No.'

Peter regarded him carefully.

'It might be, of course, that nothing further will happen. The blackmailer might cry off. On the other hand–'

'I'm worried,' said Prudhoe miserably. 'If Marjie finds out, God knows what'll happen. She's got a weak heart, you know.'

It was not for Peter to moralise. Prudhoe wanted something other than a sermon. Yet there was little that Peter could say: the man's next step was obvious.

'You haven't been to the police?'

'I can't do that,' cried Prudhoe. 'You know what the letter says.'

'But once you start paying–'

'Marjie mustn't know.'

'Mr Prudhoe, your best bet is to go to the police. They'll ensure that as much anonymity as is possible will cloak–'

'Marjie mustn't know,' repeated Prudhoe stubbornly. 'If the police don't find this … this swine she'll be told, as soon as he knows the police are looking for him.'

'All right,' considered Peter. 'Your only other course is to await developments – and think about who this blackmailer could possibly be. What about Miss Varley?'

'Please!'

It was quite remarkable the way that Prudhoe sprang to the girl's defence. It was obvious to Peter that the most positive result of the liaison had been that the girl had generated a certain affection in Prudhoe; an affection that might be overridden by his regard and fear for his wife, but which nevertheless prevented him from harbouring any suspicion that the girl herself might be trying to cash in further on the affair.

'Well, who else would be likely to know enough about the matter to be able to blackmail you?'

'Hell, I don't know! We were careful – London trips were usually business trips. I don't recall seeing anyone we knew. Around here, we usually went to pretty lonely spots. It had to be that way.'

'No jealous boy-friends of Miss Varley who might be getting their own back?'

Prudhoe's cheeks wobbled when he shook his head.

'Shouldn't think so. Susan tended to play the field. We had this ... arrangement, but there were others. I don't think I was cutting anyone's throat. As I said ... it was just an arrangement, a business arrangement if you like, between the two of us.'

Peter shrugged.

'Well, Mr Prudhoe, I suggest you wait for a while and hope this blows over. But as soon as you hear from this person – I hope you don't, but if you do – get in touch with me at once. We'll take it from there. In the meanwhile, try not to worry.'

Though that, he knew, was easier said than done.

Prudhoe agreed to leave the letter in Peter's custody. Peter stared at it curiously for a while. He wondered whether it was an isolated case – or whether there was more of it going on. It looked pretty amateurish, really. The paper was of quite good quality, though of a kind commonly sold in most stationery shops. The use of a typewriter

171

wasn't too clever because that could conceivably be traceable.

He pushed the letter inside a file cover and marked it with Prudhoe's name. He'd better not let Betty have the handling of that file. It would have to join the files which he kept separate from the general office folders. There were a number of stories in those files which could cause problems if they were to be casually glanced at by an office girl.

Even by Joan.

He dismissed the thought of Joan from his mind and attended to the papers on his desk. He worked through till lunch-time before he came up against a problem that was going to require some thought. It would seem that one of the big oil companies had lent money to a local garage to enable them to expand their premises some years before. As part of the agreement there had been a clause tying the garage to supplying only that oil company's petrol. The garage proprietor wanted to know whether he was bound by this tying agreement – now that the price war was hotting up and he could get more favourable terms from another supplier. Peter was pretty sure that he had read something about such clauses recently in the law reports. He'd have to think about it. Over lunch.

He decided on a quick snack at the Bull.

Perhaps it was the chatter in the smoke-room which prevented him from concentrating, but he was unable to recall precisely the case he wanted. He'd have to look it up when he got back. And that would mean a bit of digging. He'd often enough had cause to rail against the inefficiency of a legal system that based its law on statutes that ran back to the twelfth century, and court decisions that may or may not have been published according to the whimsical decision of a court reporter as to whether the case was important or not. When one allied to this the fact that it was not difficult for a solicitor or counsel to miss an important reported decision in an abstruse problem, it was hardly surprising that the Court of Appeal and House of Lords had more on their plates than they could digest, and that laymen (as well as lawyers) called for law reform.

What was that case he and John had spent so much time on last year? Ah, yes: Old Fletcher, at the farm in Cardington – he had bought 70 ewes on hire-purchase from a finance company, sold them to his son without disclosing the facts of hire-purchase, then defaulted on his payments. The problem was that when the finance company took back the ewes lambing time had come and gone – and there were then 67 ewes and 74 lambs. John and Peter had to convince the court that the lambs belonged not to the finance company but to young Fletcher. It was Peter who went burrowing back into Blackstone, and it was John who had triumphantly prepared the brief for counsel, drawing the distinction between a sale and a lease: for the hire-purchase agreement was classified as a lease. They'd convinced the court: Fletcher had to relinquish the ewes, for they were 'leased' and therefore owned by the company, but could hang on to the lambs – for they were 'owned' by Old Fletcher when he'd sold them to his son. But the time they'd spent on that one and the agonies they'd gone through delving into Roman and Roman-Dutch law…

And he remembered the cry of delight from Jeannette when Fletcher's wife had come round at Christmas with the fowl and the wine. 'For winning that there case for us…'

Peter realised with a start that since ten o'clock that morning his mind had dwelt neither on Jeannette, nor Billy Sneed, nor the Gaines trust.

Nor on Shirley.

He took his time going back to the office. The sun was warm on the back of his neck; the girls were in light summer dresses. It was all so normal – apart from the occasional glance that came his way. It could have been the discolouration of his face that drew their eyes, but he was inclined to guess it was more than that. They knew him by sight, or knew of him.

In a couple of weeks he would be out of this town.

And away from Shirley.

He ran up the stairs to the office. He slumped in a chair and phoned upstairs for the 1965 and 1966 Law Reports. The junior informed him that Mr Daly was using them. Peter hesitated; it might be quicker to ask John first – he might well remember the case. He rang through to John's office. Penny, John's secretary, answered.

'Oh, Mr Marlin, he's just on the way down to you. He should be there by now.'

As if on cue, John Sainsby tapped and entered the room.

'Ah, John, come in – just the man I want to see! I'm stuck on a reference: wasn't there a case on *solus* agreements recently, last two years or so? Tied garage – mortgage–'

John Sainsby's narrow eyes were thoughtful; he stroked his precise moustache with a delicate hand.

'The Harper case,' he murmured. 'Garage owner tied to one petrol supplier for twenty-one years, the supplier making a loan secured by mortgage and repayable over that period. Now then ... the House of Lords held that the tying clause was unreasonable and oppressive – not a reasonable protection of the supplier's interest. Harper's could redeem the mortgage and be free of the tie, but would remain subject to the tie until such time as they did redeem. Why? You have something similar?'

Peter explained briefly.

'Ahuh,' commented John, looking pleased with himself. 'That's the one – I think you'll find the details in the '67 All E.R. *Esso Petroleum Co., Ltd., v Harper's Garage (Stourport) Ltd.*'

'Can't tell me the page?' commented Peter in amused tones.

'I'm sorry, no,' replied his partner. He seemed hardly aware of Peter's amusement, and from the look on his face it would seem that he was already grappling with some other problem. It soon came out.

'Stephen came in to see you this morning, didn't he– about the partnership?'

Peter nodded and told him what had happened. John shook his head.

'You should have got more than that. I recommended–'

Loyalty to Stephen made his voice die away, but it was a loyalty that caused him some anguish, obviously. He couldn't look Peter in the eye: Peter had been his partner too, and they had had more in common than John and Stephen, in spite of the blood tie. Even so, over the years, John had become accustomed to being overruled and guided by Stephen and it was perhaps too late to change now.

'You haven't told Stephen yet,' said Peter quietly.

'That I'm leaving? No.'

'When are you going to tell him? You haven't changed your mind?'

'No, I've not changed my mind. I'll be telling him soon – it'll *have* to be soon anyway.'

'I don't follow you.'

'It doesn't matter,' shrugged John.

'I still think you're nuts – and Stephen will use harsher words. He'll have told you that he's expecting to be – ah – elevated, as he puts it.'

'Yes. I'm pleased for him. It's what he wanted.'

'He won't have much time for the firm then.'

'He'll get a couple of assistants, no doubt. Some youngsters who'd love to sit under a title.' John brushed nervously at some non-existent fluff on his dark grey suit. 'Did I see Mr Prudhoe in the office? What did he want?'

'Baring his soul,' sighed Peter. 'He's in trouble.'

'What kind?'

'Blackmail.'

The room was suddenly still. John's eyes flared and he went pale.

'He – he showed you a letter?'

In surprise, Peter tossed him the Prudhoe file which still lay on his desk.

'Yes – it's in here. Take a look. Not very pleasant.'

Sainsby seemed unwilling to touch it. With a distinct effort he opened the file and extracted the letter. He read it briefly, then seemed to pull himself together somewhat. He thrust the letter back and closed the file.

'Nasty,' he commented.

'Makes you wonder,' said Peter thoughtfully, watching John with care. 'This town, what is it, 40,000 people? Less, I imagine. Yet there could be a murderer here. And it would seem now a blackmailer too.'

'I don't like the offence of demanding money by threats,' said John slowly. 'In my opinion it's the most despicable of crimes.'

'You'll see plenty of it at the Bar.'

John Sainsby shook his head.

'No, I shall stay in the Chancery field. I've already written to Lincoln's Inn. Have you decide what you'll do when you leave?'

'Not yet. Take a holiday, perhaps. It's a long time since I've had one.'

'Yes … I haven't even asked how you are after the attack the other night.'

'Fine – you'll have got the details of the story from the others.'

'It's all around the town,' John said. 'You've no idea who your assailant was?'

'None.'

John looked unhappy and began to walk to the door; half-way there he stopped and looked nervously to Peter.

'Do you mind if I – take another look at that Prudhoe letter? Take it upstairs with me?'

'No, sure, take it – but for God's sake don't mislay it. And if you get any ideas, let me know.'

'Ideas?'

'About the blackmailing swine who wrote it, of course.'

It wasn't until after John had left with the letter that Peter realised what the expression on John's face really signified.

He was frightened.

3

Mrs Gaines sat in the window seat over-looking the lawns and flower-beds at Grey-gables. It had been a summer day like this when William had died; she remembered the spreading honeysuckle against the south wall, and the hum of bees – they were the first realities that had returned to her after the initial shock of the news.

It was such a long time ago.

He would have coped so much better than she; he would have been able to manage the family affairs so much more efficiently, he would have been able to talk to Sam, reason with him, form his character in a way that she would never be able to do.

Mrs Gaines sighed. She knew she was regarded as an extremely capable woman and she supposed she was, but it had been a strain – it was still a strain – attempting to shoulder the burdens alone. If only William had lived. If only–

She saw Sam stroll across the lawn; his hands were deep thrust in his pockets, his shoulders bowed as he looked down to the turf, his fair hair falling over his eyes. Was she too lenient with the boy? If she had been stricter he might have been less inclined to waste his time at the country club and car rallies, gallivanting all over the two counties, keeping all hours. She might then have been able to avoid the terrible incident last year, when Sam had collided with that other young man late one Saturday night – there had been trouble over that, they had taken him to the police station for beating the other man severely. They agreed that he had been provoked, but she felt that it was out of respect for her that they had finally brought no charges against him. That, and the fact that the other man was a local thug, a known trouble-maker. But they had hinted that the man – no, she wouldn't think that, or accept it. It was Sam's love of cars that was half the trouble. One of these days he'd kill himself in a car: she'd often told him that, cynically, but in the quiet of the night, in her bed, it caused her a real fear.

He was all that was left to her since William died. He was her only son.

And she was worried about him. He had a gay, quick disposition normally, but of late he had become introspective. She knew what the trouble was: not the meagreness of the allowance she gave him – that was a traditional complaint that had never really affected his cheerfulness. No, it was the trust holding. He had tried to tell her, several times, that there was something going on that he didn't like. She had insisted that it could wait until the next trustees' meeting. He wanted the meeting to be soon.

Of course he could be right. But she had more faith in her own judgment. She had known Peter Marlin as a child, watched him grow, and had recognised the difference he had made to the firm of Martin, Sainsby and Sons. She had every confidence in him as a solicitor to the trust. And if he said that it was necessary to support the takeover by Amalgamated Industries Ltd., she was inclined to take him at his word.

Sam was not. He had insisted that there was – to use his words – 'something fishy' going on. He had told her of the glance he had intercepted between Marlin and the man who would be taking a seat on the newly constituted board of Noble and Harris. He had told her of his own attempts to discover more of this man, this man Jackson. He had told her that he was convinced that there was some connection – 'fraudulent connection' he had said – between Jackson and Marlin. She could not believe it. Her judgment cried out against it.

She knew Peter Marlin almost as well as she knew her own son.

That had angered Sam. He'd gone off to London the next day. To City House and the Companies Registry. And two days ago John Sainsby had come out to the house and had spent a long time in the study with Sam.

Mrs Gaines did not care for John Sainsby. There was something about him, his carefulness, his precision perhaps, which offended her, stiffened her back.

But it would be simplest to write to him now; now that Peter Marlin would be leaving the firm.

She rose. She felt old. It was such a long time since William had died. Perhaps it would not be long before she joined him. Then everything would be Sam's. She hoped he would order his life wisely. He could still do so, if he kept the trust going – though Peter Marlin had advised her that once she died Sam, as sole beneficiary and of full age, would be entitled to bring the trust to an end and do as he wished with the holding.

She had once thought that Peter Marlin would be able to exercise the kind of influence over Sam that would have prevented a foolish frittering away of the holding. But Marlin had his own troubles ... and would be leaving. She wondered whether John Sainsby could ever have such an influence over her son.

When she wrote the name on the envelope she could not understand why, involuntarily, she shuddered.

4

John Sainsby returned the Prudhoe letter on Friday afternoon, without comment. But he produced two other verbal bombshells.

'I had a letter this morning, from Mrs Gaines. She suggests that since you'll shortly be leaving the firm and will obviously be unable to continue as solicitor to the Gaines trust holdings it might be a good idea that I take over in your place. Obviously, she doesn't know that I – I will probably be leaving soon.'

Peter stared at him, his pulse quickening.

'What – what are you going to do?'

John looked surprised. He ran the fingers of his left hand nervously around the inside of his right shirt-cuff.

'Well, do as she suggests, I suppose. I – well,

183

I don't want Stephen to know just yet that I will be going and he's likely to ask questions if I suggest that *he* take it on. Besides, he's so full of his damned honours stuff at the moment that he wouldn't think of looking at the Gaines file. Anyway, look, Peter, just let me have the papers and I'll take a look at them over the week-end, then we can both go along to the trustees' meeting next Tuesday–'

'Next Tuesday!'

Sainsby was startled.

'Yes – what's the matter? She wants a meeting next Tuesday, and I gather Sam – Mr Gaines – is going to raise the question of the takeover by–'

'Is he, be damned,' said Peter grimly. 'The blasted thing is all but through!'

Sainsby shrugged.

'Well, I know nothing about it all, of course, but if you'll let me have the file–'

'I've not got the stuff here at the office,' lied Peter.

'Oh? Well, when it's convenient.'

Peter was conscious of John's narrow eyes upon him. Casually, he rose to his feet.

'I took them home ... er ... last week, to do some work on them after the Noble and Harris meeting. Best thing I can do, I think, is to let you have them on Monday.'

'All right,' said John Sainsby slowly. 'Perhaps you wouldn't mind sticking in some explanatory memoranda also.'

184

'What do you mean?' asked Peter sharply.

'Eh? Well, you know, a sort of summary of recent transactions so I know what you're all talking about when we go to the meeting together. If I'm to take over from you–'

'Yes, yes.' Peter ran his hand through his hair. 'I'm sorry I jumped at you like that.'

Sainsby was still eyeing him carefully.

'That's all right, Peter. It's all been a bit of a strain, I'm sure. First, well, Jeannette, then this man Sneed, and the attack upon you. What's Inspector Crow doing about it all, anyway?'

'Damn all, if you ask me.'

'Still, suppose he knows his job. All right Peter, let me have the file on Monday and we'll go along together on Tuesday morning. I won't meet you here; it'll be more convenient if we drive out separately. I'll see you there.'

He turned on his heel and started to march out of the room. Almost as an afterthought he added:

'Seems like everyone is leaving now – you, Joan, me, and Stephen too in a sense. I was surprised to hear that Shirley Walker was leaving the area, though.'

'What! Wait, John, what's that you said? Shirley Walker? What do you mean – leaving; where's she going?'

'I thought you'd know – I mean–' Sainsby was flustered. 'She rang me yesterday and asked me to prepare a lease for her–'

'A lease!'

'That's right. She's going to let her house to a woman who lives close by. Three years, with an option to purchase. As far as I can gather, she intends leaving the district.'

'But what about her job?'

'Didn't think to ask her.'

Peter thought furiously.

He spent a wretched week-end.

He tried to telephone Shirley again, twice, with no success. It was obvious that she had gone away for the weekend. He tried to stop thinking about her, and why she had said nothing to him, and what her reasons for leaving might be. When he did manage to thrust her to the back of his mind, it was only for the Gaines matter to intrude.

The meeting would be on Tuesday.

And John would want a memorandum.

He sat gnawing at the problem for hours. If he told them everything there could be problems – perhaps not from Mrs Gaines so much as from Sam. The man had a streak of cupidity that might make things difficult. Even so...

And John. Peter would have to play it fair with John. He would have to lay it on the line, explain the whole series of transactions to him, describe in detail Peter's part in the affair – and hope that John would see things the way he saw them, and not let too many cats out of the bag.

If it hadn't been for Jeannette, none of this would have arisen...

On Sunday morning Peter took a long walk, outside the town. It was a clear, fresh morning and there were few people about on the stretch of heathland that he chose. The grass was sparkling and his shoes were quickly soaked. It was strange how catastrophically his life and his career had changed during the last few months. There had been a time when the thought of leaving would have been unthinkable, and now Jeannette was dead, fingers pointed at him in the streets, the partnership was being dissolved, and he was worrying himself to death over the Gaines trust.

And Shirley.

He lunched in a pub on the outskirts of the town: he seemed to eat out in a lot of pubs these days. When he got back to the house he had reached his decision. He would have to tell John everything.

He brought the typewriter down from Jeannette's room and inserted a blank sheet of paper. It stared at him for fully five minutes before he touched the keys.

'Dear John.'

He was no typist, and one of the keys – the *a* – seemed to be damaged, and was sticking, which didn't help. Even so, when he had finished there were four typewritten sheets of his explanation to John. He read them through quickly, felt dissatisfied at the way in which he had described his situation, thought briefly of rewriting the whole thing and then quickly typed John's name on an envelope, thrust the sheets inside and sealed it.

He'd hand it to him in the office to-morrow.

The rest of the day he spent going through the Gaines papers. There were a large number of documents there which he had no intention of handing over: they represented days of work for him, and they would hardly be relevant to John's trusteeship. Peter stored them away separately, and then read carefully right through the whole history of the Gaines holdings. It was familiar stuff – but it represented time to him, time well spent.

He had a great deal to lose – and so did the Gaines family, if the deal fell through at the last moment.

He tried to ring Shirley again on Monday morning, at her home, but there was no reply. After coffee in the office he rang the library, but a frosty chief librarian said that Miss Walker was working and personal calls were not allowed, unless they related to 'family bereavement and such like.' His call hardly fell into that category, so he rang off. He would have to attempt to intercept her after the library closed.

When he rang through to John's office, Penny answered.

'Mr John? No, he won't be in this morning, Mr Marlin. I understand he has an appointment with Mr Gaines at Greygables for eleven, but I expect him this afternoon.'

'All right, thank you, Penny. I'll come up if you ring me the moment he comes in, please.'

'Surely, Mr Marlin.'

Peter finally dealt with Mrs Davies and the question of possession of the house owned by her husband. He'd left her two months previously, and had recently attempted to sell it. She'd got wind of the sale and had come to Peter. He had already delayed longer than he should have done: the woman had three children, and was probably extremely worried about the whole thing. He drafted the letter and sent it down for typing. It was inconvenient having only one of the juniors for a secretary. Still, it was hardly worthwhile for the firm to employ another girl now, while Joan was away. John had said yesterday that Joan was leaving, but Peter had not yet heard anything official.

The day dragged on. At three-thirty he finished preparing the lease according to the instructions Shirley had given to John. He went up to John's office.

'Sorry, Mr Marlin,' said Penny brightly,

'He's not back yet.'

'I see. Look, Penny, when he does come in will you give him this note? I've got to go out now, but it's possible that he'll want to have a word with me about it so will you tell him that I'll have taken the lease around to Miss Walker? And if he can't get hold of me at home, he might try her number.'

'Certainly.' Penny smirked. Peter could almost see her mind racing away at the possibilities. He had no doubt that he had been the cause of a great deal of coffee gossip inside the office and out. It mattered little: it would soon be over.

He took the car from the customary side street parking spot and drove across town. This time he was lucky. He arrived at the library just two minutes before it was due to close, and waited for Shirley.

He stepped out of the car and stood there. She caught sight of him almost immediately, and with a quick word she left the young woman to whom she was talking and came across to him. Her face was stiff.

'Hallo, Peter,' she said quietly.

'Let's go and have a cup of tea,' he suggested. It was perhaps the greatest effort he had made in his life, but it reassured her and she softened. He suspected that she had been a little afraid of his reactions.

They took tea in a small restaurant in town. It was fairly crowded, but only one or two women appeared to recognise them. They had little to say to each other, beyond inanities concerning the weather, the library and the office. It was not until they were in the car, and almost at Shirley's home that she broke the truce.

'I imagine John Sainsby will have told you?'

Peter swung the car into the drive.

'Yes. I took the work over from him, when he told me.'

'Why?'

'So that I'd have a reason, and an excuse, for insisting upon seeing you again – at least once before you went. I've got the lease with me in the briefcase now.'

'You expected me to refuse to see you?'

Peter shrugged, and killed the idling engine.

'You hadn't told me that you were thinking of leaving.'

She opened the car door and got out.

'You'd better come inside, Peter.' She led the way, fumbling in her handbag for the key. 'The fact is that it all came up rather suddenly. Mrs Taylor, across the way there had ... had heard about the difficulties at the library and since her son is shortly getting married she wondered whether I'd be leaving the area, and perhaps selling or leasing the house. It went on from there and was quickly settled.'

'What about the difficulties at the library?'

Almost unconsciously, Shirley slung the coat she was carrying on top of the books she had dumped on a chair in the hallway. She led the way into the sitting-room. Reluctantly, she replied, 'I finish there at the end of the month.'

'But why?'

'Why are *you* leaving your firm?'

'Yes, but surely–'

'My dear Peter, don't be so naïve. Can't you imagine what a furore there was when … when Jeannette died? There had already been talk, and Potter's remarks at the coroner's inquest only hardened attitudes that had already been formed. The chief librarian had already had a word with me about our association, a long time before that.'

'You're not serious!'

'I am, and so was he. He thought a member of his staff should be a very Caesar's wife.'

Peter was silent for a moment. He sat down.

'I'm sorry, Shirley,' he said finally.

She laughed, shortly.

'Don't be ridiculous. I'm all grown up, you know. I suppose I'd been half expecting it really, ever since I met you. I mean, after all, it was bound to have repercussions wasn't it? You were a married man.'

Not any longer, he thought.

'I tried to phone you over the week-end.'

'I got a taxi to pick me up at the library on Friday. I stayed with a girl-friend in London. Hen talk. Crying on each other's shoulder. She's had man trouble too. It seems that none of the men she meets are attractive *and* single. I know what she means. It can be quite a problem for a girl.'

'Shirley – I'm sorry about the way things have turned out. Truly sorry.'

'You've said it. So now forget it. If it's any consolation, I'm sorry too, but what the heck! It's not the end of the world.'

Her breeziness failed to cover the obvious effort she was making to be cheerful. It depressed him. He fell silent. The last months had been mental agony for him: the pressures had been too numerous, and too heavy. He felt that he had become almost an automaton; he no longer really knew what was important and what was not. Gaines, Shirley, the firm, Jeannette ... Jeannette. Time was when she would have come first in the list.

Shirley was staring at him. He forced a grin.

'No, I don't suppose it is the end of the world, is it?'

She didn't react. She had fallen serious too.

'Peter, you're worried about something. God knows, we've both got enough to worry

about with Jeannette's death and its implications and then that poor Sneed, but
there's more, isn't there?'

'How do you mean?'

'Is it Paul Jackson?'

'I don't understand.'

'At the booking-office, with Inspector
Crow, you told me that you'd recognised
that man – and then you seemed to be sorry
that you'd said it. And you've not mentioned it since – not that you've seen me
since, but on the way back, I mean. What is
there about Jackson?'

'Oh ... it's nothing, Shirley. It's, well, it
concerns the Gaines trust.'

'And it's worrying you.'

Peter shrugged.

'Yes, it is. I'll be relinquishing the trusteeship now, of course: the new trust deed will
appoint John Sainsby.'

'But what difference does that make?'

'It's a long story,' said Peter slowly. Too
long, and too irrelevant to Shirley's problems to bore her with it. Yet he felt the need
to tell someone, someone he could trust, get
the whole thing off his chest. He'd kept it
bottled up – and Jackson ... what the hell
was Jackson up to? What had he been doing
in the booking-hall? Was it mere coincidence
that he'd been there? Surely he couldn't have
been concerned with that locker! It was
absurd ... there was no connection ... and

194

yet, why had he been so shifty, so evasive as to pretend not to see Peter and shy off like a startled colt?

'Why don't you tell me all about it?' asked Shirley quietly. 'It may help.'

Perhaps it would.

'When William Gaines died he left a trust fund, largely comprising shares in Noble and Harris, the textile firm. There are three trustees now: me, Sam Gaines, who's also a beneficiary, after his mother, and Byrne, the accountant. About two years ago I decided something had to be done about Noble and Harris...

'You see, Shirley, a firm sometimes gets into difficulty by trying to meet a demand beyond its own resources. Good management can prevent it, but the directors of Noble and Harris are not good managers: they had expanded too fast, and although they couldn't see the danger signs they really needed more capital to cover the dangers of non-liquidity – they'd relied on too much short-term borrowing, over-trading in relation to their own long-term capital.

'They wouldn't listen when I raised it at the annual general meeting and Byrne wouldn't back me. I could see the Gaines shares would be going downhill. The only way they could avoid disaster would be to approach a financially stronger company with a view to sale or amalgamation.'

'And they wouldn't do it?'

'They were completely hostile to the idea.'

Peter shrugged.

'What could I do?' he continued. 'See the trust holdings become worthless? Sam Gaines was too thick to see what was happening, Byrne too old, the firm too obstructive in its attitudes to act. Then I met Paul Jackson. At one of Jeannette's parties…'

'What happened?'

'Nothing at first. But I knew that he was a company man, and able to raise money with his connections in the City. So when I had worked out the plan and sweated months on the files I knew we could do it. Amalgamated Industries Ltd. was formed, with capital provided by Jackson, and an offer was made for the Noble and Harris shares. It was accepted by over ninety per cent of the shareholders at the general meeting – a close thing, mind, but it was accepted, and it's now going through. The shareholders could take cash, or shares in Amalgamated Industries in return for their holdings.'

Shirley lit two cigarettes, passed him one, and tucked her legs under her as she sat in the chair opposite him.

'But how does this give the trust an advantage?'

'Jackson knows everything about Noble and Harris. He knows just what to do. He will pump some more capital into the firm –

where it will pay off – and he will sell those assets of the firm which are a drag on its business. The resultant capital can be distributed: I've calculated that the value of the trust holding will rise considerably within the next two years.'

'But that's marvellous, Peter! I don't see what you're worried about! The Gaines family certainly can't cavil about that – they stand to gain!'

Peter's face was grim.

'Sam suspects that there's some fraudulent dealing going on.'

'But that's surely nonsense!'

'I'm afraid,' said Peter slowly, 'that it's not. At least, not entirely.'

Shirley stared at him with round eyes. One hand brushed back a dark strand of hair.

'What you've told me – there's no fiddle there, surely!'

'It's not exactly a fiddle,' replied Peter uneasily. 'But you see, Shirley, there might be trouble. I didn't tell you the whole story. I said that Amalgamated Industries will take over. I didn't tell you that Amalgamated Industries is a holding company. And Paul Jackson is my nominee.'

Shirley swung her legs down, and leant forward.

'You mean *you* own some shares in Amalgamated Industries!'

'More than *some,*' growled Peter. 'I've

used Paul as a nominee but I've got a big holding.'

'And if the Gaines trust holding does well out of this, *you* also will do well. Personally.'

'Exactly. And Sam Gaines will make something out of that.' Peter drew nervously at the cigarette: he was briefly aware that Shirley's lips had touched it. 'But worse, if anything goes wrong – if Sam tries to pull back, I'm in trouble. You see, I didn't have the money to float the holding company: Paul Jackson lent it to me.'

And at the booking-office he had tried to avoid me, thought Peter. Shirley was looking at him doubtfully.

'But you've still done nothing which–'

'At the very least,' said Peter harshly, 'it could be said I've acted unethically. And Sam Gaines will say it, I've no doubt, to-morrow. At the worst...' He shrugged. 'Anyway, I've told John all about it, in a letter to-day. I don't really want to talk about it any more, Shirley.'

'I understand.'

She got up.

'You want me to get the lease now?' he asked miserably.

She shook her head. Her tone was decided.

'No. To hell with the lease for the time being. I'm going to the bedroom Peter, to change. While I'm getting ready, I would suggest that you pour a drink for yourself. Then we shall sit down for an hour and play some restful music and then you are going to take me out for a drive, and a meal later, and to hell with everything and everyone.' She paused, looking down at him. 'Do you think that's a good idea?'

'I think it's a marvellous idea.'

'That's it, then. But no strings, Peter. We're doing this because we've been too miserable, too tense, too much under pressure, we like each other, and it's time we took the occasion to relax. But it's no more than that. You agree?'

'I agree.'

And yet, when he searched through the records that Shirley had stacked in the corner of the room, he wondered. Did he agree? Was it as simple as that? Could it be as cool, and easy as that? There had been a time when such an attitude between them would have been an impossibility. Had they changed so much since then?

He came across some of Shirley's tapes – and others he recognised. He'd brought them over, the night after the coroner had delivered himself of that appalling speech in court. There was one tape he particularly liked … something he had once taped himself from a radio programme. It wasn't there. Never mind – this unmarked one would do – it would indeed, he thought. It was an orchestrated version of some light music. Jeannette must have taped it at some time. The soft music swelled out and he turned the volume down slightly, then poured himself a drink.

He dropped to the settee, with the drink in his hand. He let his mind wash free of thought. The music swirled around him. Ten minutes later Shirley came in. He rose and poured her a drink, without speaking. When she took it from him he looked at her. Her eyes were bright and as they stood close together she seemed to have difficulty with her breathing. Her lips were slightly parted and he realised that after all–

'Shirley–' he began, reaching out to hold her.

And the music stopped, and someone was laughing.

It was Jeannette.

5

'Play it again,' said Peter harshly.

'Peter–'

'Play it again!'

Shirley stared at him for a long moment, then with a shrug she went across to the tape-recorder. Her face was pale. There was the sound of whirring tape, back-tracking. Then the soft music stole through the room again. Shirley looked back to him, appealingly. He ignored her. He was waiting.

In a moment there came the click ... and the sound of Jeannette's laughter. With a masochistic fascination Peter listened.

'...you don't mind me turning this thing off. It's something I taped from that ghastly "Tea at Three" programme this afternoon, and I was just playing it again when I heard you at the door. There, I'll just put it on rewind... Now then, Stephen, can I get you a drink?'

Stephen Sainsby's quiet clipped tones came across faintly.

'That would be very pleasant, Jeannette. I ... I gather Peter isn't at home?'

'I'm afraid not, Stephen. He's still at the office – he must have something, or *someone* on tap there, it seems to me. He told me he'd be particularly late to-night. You wanted to see him, specially?'

'Well, yes, but it's nothing that can't wait. If I may say so,' Stephen added slowly, 'I'd much rather see you, anyway.'

The way Jeannette laughed made Peter flinch. It was not the fact that she laughed; it was the quality of her laughter. It had a provocative meaning that was painfully obvious.

'Well really, Stephen, that was most gallant of you. In a moment I'll be suspecting that you came round here knowing damn' well that Peter wouldn't be home this evening!'

'You know very well, my dear, that this wouldn't be too far from the truth.'

'Now why on earth should you do that?' Jeannette was asking sweetly.

'You bitch!'

Stephen Sainsby's tone was admiring.

'After the way you behaved last week, Jeannette, you can still put on an act for me? You made it perfectly obvious that–'

'That what, Stephen?'

There was a huskiness in her voice now, a huskiness that was familiar to Peter. It had always attracted him, it always told him that her sexuality was aroused. He knew now that it had never been anything but an affectation, something she could turn on at will. Agonised, he listened. There was a rustling sound…

'Peter!' Shirley came forward to him, with her hand outstretched anxiously. 'Please turn it off.'

'No,' he said harshly, pulling her down beside him on the settee. Jeannette was speaking again, breathlessly.

'Really, Stephen, if Peter should return now–'

Stephen Sainsby's reply was urgent.

'He won't return, not yet a while, but Jeannette, for God's sake, can't we do something about this? Last week, and now tonight, you're damned well tormenting me. If

I don't have you–'

'Yes?' Caressingly.

'Can't we fix something up? I have to get up to London soon. Can't we...?'

'I've already spent rather a long time in London, Stephen, wouldn't you say?'

'I can get a flat,' Sainsby was saying eagerly. 'If you can get away for a couple of weeks–'

'Only a couple of weeks?'

'Well, as long as you like, Jeannette. Longer the better. Leave him, if you like, I'll look after you. I'll–'

'You'll what, darling?'

'You tantalising witch–'

The sounds were unmistakable. Peter felt sick. He realised that he was gripping Shirley's hand fiercely. Her face was white.

He was aware then only of odd sounds. Through a haze of whirling memories and mingled disgust Peter heard her arranging to meet Stephen, heard her urge him to leave then before her husband returned, heard her whispered good-bye.

And her final contemptuous remark after Sainsby had gone.

'Would you have guessed the old stallion had it in him?'

After that, there was only the whispering sound of the whirring tape.

Shirley rose quietly and walked across to switch off the machine. The room was silent. Pale evening sunshine drifted through dancing dust specks.

'Peter–'

He began to laugh. Quietly at first, then more loudly. It had a cynical ring.

'D'you know,' he sputtered, 'Stephen Sainsby was talking to me, only last Friday. He was turning over to me a sad little man who'd been sleeping around and who was terrified that his wife would find out. You know what my senior partner said? He said that there are things one can and can not do. That a man should live a decent life. That it takes little to behave in a responsible manner. *He* said that. To *me!*'

'Peter, I'm sorry – what can I say?'

'And you should have seen the look on his face. Disgusted, outraged morality! And all the time–'

Shirley dropped to her knees beside him, and took his hand. She was near to tears.

'Peter, please… I think you should forget it.'

'Forget it? How the hell can I forget it? Don't you realise, Shirley, how it was with me and Jeannette? I loved her. She was expensive, but I loved her and I worked like a bloody slave for her. More than that – I threw over my professional standards for her. Don't you realise why I was so worried about the Amalgamated Industries thing? Because I knew all along I was sticking my neck out – but I'd gone too far to back out.

But I needed money, I needed to make money – for her! That's why I closed my eyes to my own professional reputation and contacted Paul Jackson. Sure, I kept telling myself that what I was doing was for the good of the trust, but all the time the *main* reason was that I wanted money. For *her!*'

His lips writhed back in a terrible grimace.

'By God, this'll put paid to his Knighthood!'

Shirley's hands fastened on his.

'Peter,' she urged, 'you – you're not going to make it public?'

He stared at her. Anger was washing away from his veins now. He felt suddenly helpless, and defeated. One by one the layers of his defences were being stripped away. First Jeannette had left him, then her return had lost Shirley for him. Jeannette had never been his thereafter, but her death had yet left him with memories of the way it had been, once upon a time. Now he knew that there had never been a time. Now he knew just what Jeannette had been.

Make it public? For what purpose? To tell everyone he had been cuckolded? Lavender would certainly hush up *his* affair with Jeannette; and Sainsby's lurking Knighthood would crush any thought of confession from the senior partner. And what would Peter have to gain? There was no point in making it public.

Everything had changed, and nothing had changed. Jeannette was dead. He had thought Lavender could have killed her. By the same criterion it could equally have been Stephen Sainsby. And who else? *Who else?*

For all he knew half the men in the two counties could have been Jeannette Marlin's lovers. She'd been nothing but a whore.

Shirley was staring at him; in her eyes there was a real distress, and he remembered what had been in her eyes the moment before Jeannette's laugh had torn across their emotions. It was all too late, now.

'It looks as though we won't be going out now,' he said quietly.

'If you say so,' she replied sadly.

'It's no good, Shirley. You see that, don't you?'

'If you say so.'

He was strangely reluctant to leave, but felt he had to. He went across to his briefcase, and extracted the lease and its counterpart. His voice was measured and flat.

'You'll execute these two documents and so will Mrs Taylor, or her son, or whoever it is. There are instructions attached. You'll hand the lease over to her; you'll keep the counterpart.' He closed his briefcase. 'If you have any problems, John will deal with them.'

Shirley was looking at him strangely.

'Is this good-bye, Peter?'

He shook his head. 'I don't know. I'm sorry, Shirley, I just can't think straight. Not now. I hope – I hope I'll see you again, before you leave.'

'Or before *you* do.' Her tone was cool. She was in control of herself now.

At the door he paused and smiled weakly at her.

'Wish me luck, for the Gaines slaughter to-morrow?'

'I wish you luck, Peter, all the luck you need.'

And I'll need it, he thought. Previously, he could at least have argued, because there had been reason for acting as he had done. Now, there was nothing. Just the realisation that it had all been for nothing – for that was what Jeannette had been. Nothing.

The telephone was ringing.

'One moment, Peter, don't go. I'll just see who it is.'

Shirley stepped back into the hallway to pick up the telephone receiver. A moment later she called out to him.

'Peter! It's for you.'

She was standing there with her hand over the mouthpiece.

'It's John Sainsby,' she said. 'He – he sounds strange.'

'He'll have received my letter,' commented Peter, 'about the Gaines transactions.'

He took the telephone from Shirley.

'Hallo, John? This is Peter. You got my letter?'

There was a brief silence. John Sainsby seemed to be having difficulty controlling his breathing. When the words came they were uncharacteristic.

'Marlin,' he gasped. 'You cynical, hypocritical bastard!'

And the line went dead.

CHAPTER VI

1

Inspector Crow remained silent for a long time as he sat behind his desk, staring at the letter which John Sainsby had presented to him. He flicked over the last sheet again. His eyes fixed on the signature. *Peter* ... a broad, confident hand. Crow returned to the first page and gazed at it, stolidly.

John Sainsby shifted nervously in his seat. There was a line of perspiration along his neat moustache and his hands were damp. The constable at his back, and the inspector facing him, obviously unnerved him completely.

Inspector Crow looked up from the letter.

'Yes,' he said heavily. 'I see what you mean.'

He sounded sad, yet resigned.

Sainsby flickered a dry tongue along his lips.

'Has – has Mr Gaines been ... in touch with you?'

His eyes were feverish. Inspector Crow placed Marlin's letter on the table, carefully, and shook his head.

'Not yet, Mr Sainsby. Though I've no doubt that he will. Now ... can you inform me where I am likely to get hold of Mr Marlin this morning?'

Sainsby looked down at his damp hands.

'He will be at Greygables by now,' he muttered. 'The trustees' meeting. I was to have attended, but when I got this letter I decided I should come straight to you.'

'Yes, I understand, Mr Sainsby. All right. Well, I think that the best thing for you to do would be to go home for the time being. There's no doubt that I will want to see you again shortly, but you're obviously more than a little upset. Leave the papers with me and I'll go out and ... have a word with Mr Marlin at once.'

'I think I'd rather return to the office,' whispered Sainsby in a strained voice.

'Just as long as you let us know where we can get in touch with you,' soothed Inspector Crow. 'Wilson, show Mr Sainsby out now. And then ask Jardine if he has managed to get those files I asked about, will you? Good-bye for the present, Mr Sainsby.'

Crow leaned back in his chair, as the door closed behind Sainsby. His physical discomfort in a chair that was too short for his long back was matched only by the mental depression that had overcome him. It really was a too bad: he had misjudged people in the past, and he would do so again. But if this letter was right, he had made a great mistake about Peter Marlin.

And yet ... there were too many yets, and too many buts. It had been an uncomfortable investigation. It had begun badly – the local police work had been sloppy, people hadn't been questioned closely enough, statements accepted almost at face value, and then there'd been Lavender and the pressure from Gray; the intrusion of his private emotions upon what should be routine matters; the silly little difficulties that the local force had put in his way; it all added up to a situation that made it almost impossible to act with the directness he liked to use. What was it they said back at headquarters– 'as the Crow flies'? It was the way he liked to work and he didn't mind the crack. But this depressing office ... he was sad.

But then, when was he happy? Martha always said he seemed to the outside world to be the unhappiest man alive. She knew better, but being married to him for twenty years she should be able to take up a position that allowed her to understand him. He was certainly happy when he was with her. She was forty now, and dumpy. He knew they made an odd physical contrast. People often smiled, sometimes laughed when they saw them together. But what did it matter? They had twenty years of a happy marriage behind them: *they* could afford to laugh at others.

Some others had unhappy marriages. Like Peter Marlin.

His head jerked up at the smart rapping on the door. It was Jardine, officious as ever.

'The records you requested, sir. Couple of photographs, too.'

'Good, thank you Jardine. I'll return them later, once I've had a good look at them.'

Once Jardine had withdrawn, Inspector Crow drew the folder towards him and glanced at the two photographs. They had been taken at the hospital. He pored over them for a long time before he turned to the reports.

It was the last few sentences of the report that particularly drew his attention. 'The abrasions were certainly the result of the initial impact. It is my considered opinion, however, that the other injuries were inflicted later. It would seem that these injuries were caused *after* the man had lost consciousness. They were the result of deliberate blows, which the unconscious man was unable to avoid.'

Crow stared at the photographs again. He felt cold. It couldn't be proved, obviously, but there was the doctor's opinion. Beaten, deliberately, after he was unconscious.

Anger stirred in Crow's veins.

It was time to see Peter Marlin.

2

Mrs Gaines was proud of her drawing-room. William had spent a great deal of money on it years ago, and it had repaid the investment. Its panelled walls had now toned down magnificently to a dull, reserved sheen that set off the splendour of the oaken table to perfection. The high french window glanced down to a lawn and stream that sent light reflections dancing on the ceiling in high summer. The green carpet had not faded noticeably over the years although, she supposed, if one looked under the bookcases that stationed themselves in military fashion against the wall one might discover a deeper tone there.

It was a room to savour, and she enjoyed the sensation now as she sat there. It was her moment, for soon the others would come in, to deal with this tiresome business of the trust. It was sad, but she feared that bitter words would fly: she did not like bitterness, not now, not at her time of life. She had taken her fill of that particular cup and wanted no more, but she knew that Sam had for some reason come to regard the dispute with Peter Marlin as a personal vendetta. Perhaps he was right. Even so, she suspected otherwise, for Peter Marlin was a capable young man, and an able solicitor, and her son, well, he was her son, but he had yet to show the determination that she knew both she and William had possessed, the sense of right, and the control of personal feelings that was so necessary if one was to make one's way in the world, and keep its respect.

William had earned respect, and, she thought, so had she. Sam was young. Perhaps he would learn, soon.

She hoped that this meeting wouldn't develop into a brawl.

She could hear their voices in the hall and she adjusted the high neck of her grey dress. They came in then, James Byrne leading the way, broad, thickening at his red jowls, peering over his glasses and smiling at her. She had known him for many years. He had once been an able accountant but of recent years he had given up the chase somewhat. Next, Peter Marlin. She hadn't realised before that his dark hair was beginning to fleck with grey. His father, she remembered, had looked far too distinguished for a farm labourer. He had been a handsome man too, more striking than Peter, she seemed to recall, but that would be because Peter's mother had had softer, more malleable features. But Peter had certainly taken his father's bold, upright stance and walk ... it was strange how the years could roll back before her.

Then Sam. How could she be objective about him? She tried so hard to be objective, but it was difficult ... he was her only son. His fair hair was straighter now than it had been when he was a child, and his narrow features were obviously coarser. But he retained a little of the grace of movement that had been his when he had been at her knee and if he had been – and still was – somewhat petulant, that must be a fault of hers. William had never displayed petulance.

'Are we ready to start, Mother?'

She looked towards James Byrne and inclined her head gracefully. As chairman, he would begin.

'Hrrumph! Well, Mrs Gaines,' rumbled Byrne, 'this meeting of the trustees has been called at the request of Mr Gaines here to discuss the matter of the ... er ... acquisition of shares in Amalgamated Industries Ltd., in place of those at present held in Noble and Harris Ltd. As I ... er ... understand the position the offer is now being taken up, and I imagine that you, Mr Gaines, are really wanting us to decide whether we, as trustees, should take up the shares, or whether we should take a cash distribution at – er – I believe it is £4 10s a share. Well, in my opinion–'

'Yes, let us have your opinion, Mr Byrne,'

cut in Sam acidly. Mrs Gaines tried to catch his eye angrily, but he refused to meet her glance. James Byrne looked a little startled.

'Yes, well, er, yes. I … er … I was saying that in my opinion we would be well advised to take the cash. The reason why I suggest this of course is that we know very little – indeed, nothing about the firm of Amalgamated Industries Ltd.–'

'Is that so?' drawled Sam.

Mrs Gaines caught the sharp glance that Peter Marlin cast in her son's direction, but listened still, for Byrne was well launched.

'…and in my experience, which you might well regard as extensive, after some forty years or more in the accountancy profession, it is pretty clear to me that we need to tread warily. It is our duty as trustees to ensure that trust moneys are not frittered away, and should we therefore decide to take up the share issue we might find that we are backing a horse which will fall dead in the shafts. There is no evidence to suppose that the firm is likely to produce the kind of trading figures that have been enjoyed in the past by Noble and Harris – figures which have been steady, I agree, rather than startling–'

'Mr Marlin,' interrupted Sam sweetly, 'is of the opinion that the firm of Noble and Harris has been in a state of atrophy for the last two years.'

'It would be more courteous,' commented Mrs Gaines mildly, 'if you were to give Mr Byrne the opportunity to finish what he is saying.'

Byrne hardly seemed to have noticed the interchange.

'–so, when all things are taken into consideration I am convinced that the best course that we, as trustees, can take is to accept the cash, make suitable safe investments and proceed from there.'

He looked around portentously.

'Now, Mr Gaines, I think you wished to make a comment.'

Sam flashed the smile that Mrs Gaines knew so well. One thing Sam had taken from William: his natural charm.

'Please,' he smiled. 'After Mr Marlin.'

Peter Marlin was holding a pencil and staring down at the papers he had placed on the table in front of him.

'You already have my recommendations,' he said quietly. 'In my opinion you should accept the offer of shares in Amalgamated Industries Ltd.'

'Would you care to elaborate upon your reasons for so recommending, Mr Marlin?' sneered Sam. Mrs Gaines was aware that the atmosphere between the two young men was becoming tense.

'I have already expressed my reasons, but, if you wish, I will repeat them,' replied Peter

Marlin. 'Noble and Harris will shortly be in financial difficulties, and only a fresh injection of capital can save them; fresh capital, and a cutting back of their present outgoings. They have two unprofitable subsidiary factories in particular which are a drain upon them. They should be excised, and a re-grouping of management and control should take place. I understand that if Amalgamated Industries take over, this will be their policy.'

'You understand?' At the sound of Sam's voice, Mrs Gaines trembled. Sam's hostility towards Peter Marlin was quite open now. 'Tell me, Marlin – what do you mean by *understand?* Where do you get the inform-ation from?'

'The papers put out by–'

'What papers? Don't talk such rubbish to me, Marlin. How well do you know Paul Jackson?'

'Jackson?' queried Mrs Gaines. Her son turned to her. His face was beginning to flush.

'Jackson, dear Mother, is the member of the board of directors of Amalgamated Industries Ltd. who will be responsible for the reorganisation of the management of Noble and Harris. He is the man who has been carrying on the negotiations. Well, Marlin, do you know him?'

'Slightly.'

'Slightly! The last time I asked you, you

218

said you didn't know him at all! What are you trying to hide, Marlin? Tell us, what are you trying to cover up?'

Peter Marlin was looking at her; Mrs Gaines saw no fear in his eyes but a certain resignation that she could not understand. He opened his mouth to speak, but her son gave him no opportunity.

'I'll damned well tell you what you're hiding, Marlin. One bloody great fiddle!'

'*Sam!*'

Mrs Gaines was aghast at the venom in Sam's tone; it was as though he hated Peter Marlin, as though the two had been lifelong enemies. She could not understand what was going on. She fixed a piercing glance on her flushed son and said, 'I think that you had better apologise to Mr Marlin.'

He shook his head. Suddenly he was smiling. It was a smile that chilled her more than his anger could have done. Suddenly she did not understand her son.

'No. I don't *need* to apologise, dear Mother. Because I'm telling the truth. I'd rather justify my remarks than apologise for them. If John Sainsby had been here this morning he could have explained it better than I, but John,' he sneered, staring at Peter Marlin, 'is otherwise engaged.'

'I don't understand,' said Mrs Gaines levelly.

'You will, Mother,' grinned Sam. 'It's all

quite simple, really. This man Jackson is a director of and major shareholder in Amalgamated Industries. He is also the nominee of our friend, Mr Peter Marlin!'

'Is this true?' pondered Byrne heavily.

'I checked at Companies House, ferreted around, had a long talk with John Sainsby. I know my facts, Byrne, believe me. Don't you see, Mother? Marlin has been using us, hoping to clean up a pile for himself!'

Mrs Gaines sighed, and turned to Peter Marlin.

'Is this true?' she asked.

'No,' he replied shortly.

Sam yelped in triumph.

'Listen to him! He's lying in his teeth! I've checked, Marlin! I know the blasted truth! You're the moving force behind this takeover and you stand to gain a hell of a lot of money!'

'Mrs Gaines.' Marlin was ignoring Sam, and addressing himself directly to her. She saw the knot of anger stir in Sam's jaw, but she listened to Marlin. 'What he says is a perversion of the truth. I believe that this takeover is necessary for the well being of Noble and Harris and for the trust holding. If it goes through, the trust holding stands to make a great deal of money. No, it *will* make a great deal of money. I'd stake my reputation on it!'

'Reputation!' screamed Sam in derision.

Marlin ignored him.

'It is perfectly true,' he continued, 'that Jackson is my nominee. It was necessary because it was he who would have to raise the necessary capital in the City, where I am not known. Confidence reposes in his ability and reputation. Moreover, he is an experienced company man and would be able to handle the delicate negotiations involved far better than I. Even so, I must emphasise that the whole thing was completely necessary for otherwise the minority investments of the trust holding would not have been looked after. This way they will, for I'm concerned – behind, if you like, the negotiations, and I know what will happen.'

'For God's sake,' snarled Sam. 'Come off your pure white horse and tell the truth! You *own* shares in Amalgamated Industries – if the takeover goes through you gain *personally.*'

'All right,' snapped Peter Marlin, his eyes blazing. 'I do – but so does the trust! And without my intervention the holding would have faded away to nothing.'

'Even so,' rumbled Byrne unhappily, 'to take a direct interest...'

'Listen!' demanded Sam Gaines. 'I told you I had a long, sometimes hypothetical talk with John Sainsby. The upshot is that we have this character over a barrel.'

'I have listened,' said Mrs Gaines quietly,

'but I am not convinced that Mr Marlin has done anything illegal. I am not sure he has acted wisely, but–'

'Wisely! He's stuck his neck out, Mother. He's a trustee – he has a fiduciary position in relation to the trust and one of his basic duties is to ensure that he does not betray the trust – which he does if he allows his personal interest to come into conflict with his duty as a trustee!'

'My personal interest,' snapped Peter, 'has in no way affected my professional judgment!'

'In a pig's eye it hasn't! You're more concerned with your rake-off than anything else! Tell me this: at the annual general meeting which we attended together recently you didn't inform me of the importance of our vote. Why not?'

'It wasn't necessary to explain it. I was doing my best for the trust–'

'For yourself, you mean! Mother, let me explain the situation to you. He *used* the trust for his own benefit! The Noble family hold about eight per cent of the shares in Noble and Harris. Like us, they are minority shareholders. Now when a company makes a takeover bid for another company, and the offer is accepted by the holders of *ninety per cent of the shares,* the company making the offer can get the rest of the shares – those belonging to the shareholders who voted against the acceptance – on the same terms. Don't you see? The offer could have been accepted by the Noble and Harris directors, but if we had stuck out with the Noble *family* Mr Peter Marlin here wouldn't have got his ninety per cent – and who knows? Maybe a few of the directors wouldn't have sold then, and where would Marlin's controlling interest be then? Gone in a puff of smoke. I tell you, Mother, it was a fiddle!'

Mrs Gaines turned to Peter Marlin, but he was already speaking.

'I congratulate you on your research, Sam,' he said quietly. 'That and no doubt your talks with John Sainsby seem to have filled you in pretty well on the background. But all that you say means nothing at all. The fact is, I have been working on this for two years. I've sweated blood over it. I think you *know* how much time I've put to it. And I'm satisfied, whatever my own private interests in the matter might be, I'm satisfied that I have worked for the trust holding, and for the best interests of the trust holding. And let me make one more point, Sam, before you interrupt – I am the only person I *have* to satisfy. It's a matter of personal integrity. I can assure you, and your mother, that I've done nothing illegal.'

'It depends what you mean by illegal,' scoffed Sam Gaines. He looked to his mother. 'And what's your reaction, darling?

You going to take his side and to hell with the trust? Or are you going to credit me with a little intelligence at last?'

Mrs Gaines's mouth hardened.

'I've always credited you with intelligence, Sam,' she snapped. 'It's simply been the matter of the application of your intelligence which has worried me.'

She turned to Peter Marlin. He met her eyes, but she was not convinced. She knew that he had put up a show this morning, but on another day he could have demolished Sam. His heart wasn't in the battle; for some reason he was not prepared to fight. He would not capitulate for capitulation was not in the man, but he had no true faith in his cause.

But did he have faith in the trust's cause?

'I want only one thing from you, Peter Marlin,' she said. 'I am of the personal opinion that you have acted unethically: you lawyers have a saying that not only must justice be done, it must be seen to be done. I see little justice, in that sense, in your statements as far as the trust is concerned and your conduct in relation to it. But what is done is done. I want, as I say, only one assurance from you. Is it your honest, professionally based belief – irrespective of personal gain – that this takeover by Amalgamated Industries will be for the long term benefit of the trust holding?'

He met her eyes unwaveringly.

'Mrs Gaines, I am *convinced* of it.'

She stared at him for a long time. Her hands, blue-veined, were still in her lap.

'I've known you for many years, Peter Marlin. I knew your father before you. On the meadows I trusted his judgment. On this, I trust you now.'

Silence fell.

'Hrrumph,' coughed Byrne. 'I suppose that talks it out. Well, nothing I've heard changes my opinion, of course—'

'Of course,' echoed Sam with a grin. His anger seemed to have evaporated.

'—and I still maintain that we should take cash. Mrs Gaines is the principal beneficiary and we are entitled and expected to take her views into account but not bound by them of course—'

'My view is Peter Marlin's view,' said Mrs Gaines quietly, without taking her eyes from the young solicitor.

'—but we will now take a vote on it. Mr Marlin?'

'I would want the trust holding to acquire shares in Amalgamated Industries rather than accept cash. The offer of £4 10s is a good one but there is more to be gained from the shares.'

'Mr Gaines?'

'Oh, my dear chap, my views are as those of my mother and Mr Marlin! Who am I to quarrel, and cross swords with the solicitor to the trust? No, shares, by all means!'

Mrs Gaines caught the glance of pure annoyance that flashed from Peter Marlin to Sam. Her son was smiling sardonically.

'So we go ahead with the transaction,' said Byrne heavily. 'The papers are all prepared – perhaps you gentlemen, as trustees, would care to add your signatures to these documents, after reading them with due care. You, of course, are already familiar with them, Mr Marlin?'

Mrs Gaines rose.

'I will order some coffee. It is a pleasant morning – perhaps we could have it on the terrace.'

She left the room and spoke to Molly, giving her the relevant instructions. When she walked out to the terrace Sam followed her. The others were still in the drawing-room, with the documents.

'Your smile,' commented Mrs Gaines with some asperity, 'denotes satisfaction. I can't understand why. Sam, you made a completely unnecessary scene this morning. And for nothing. What was the point of all that argument if, at the end of it, you were going to *agree* to Mr Marlin's suggestions – albeit an agreement couched in offensive terms?'

'Mother, I delight in your phrasing. There is something so tremendously Victorian about it. But you're wrong. I didn't do it all for nothing. You see, I imagine that Peter Marlin is absolutely right in his assessment of the financial situation. But I'm damned if I was going to allow him to get away with thinking that he could pull the wool over my eyes! I wanted him to realise that I was on to his little game.'

He smiled again. Mrs Gaines felt it was not a pleasant smile to observe.

'Moreover,' added Sam, 'I didn't disclose all that I have gleaned from John Sainsby. The fact is, Mother dear, Peter Marlin might have bought those shares, but he'll never make a penny out of the transaction.'

Mrs Gaines glanced up to her son, as he stood rocking with his hands behind his back, gazing up at the pale sun.

'I don't understand. If he owns the shares—'

Sam shook his head.

'He owns them all right *but* – and it's a very big but. All that legal nonsense I talked about the trustee having a duty to the trust is true, but there's more to it than that. There's another rule which says – a *trustee cannot profit from the trust.*'

'But he's not making a profit from the trust,' puzzled Mrs Gaines. 'From the shares in Amalgamated Industries, yes, but his shares are not *trust* shares.'

'Mother dear, leave it to sonny boy. Of course they're not trust shares. But where did he get the information which led to his deciding to buy up Noble and Harris? From the firm itself. In what capacity was he acting when he was given access to that information? The capacity of trustee. How did he use the knowledge gained? To buy shares in Amalgamated Industries for the trust – *and for himself.* In short, Mother mine, he used information obtained while acting as trustee to reap a secret benefit for himself. And that is nothing more than breach of his fiduciary duty – which means he'll have to account to us for every penny he gets!'

'You mean,' said Mrs Gaines slowly, 'that if we made money on the shares, as he says we *all* will, we could demand that he pay his profits to us?'

'Exactly.'

Mrs Gaines stared at her son. There had been times of late when she felt that he was growing away from her, when she felt she could no longer understand him. But she understood what she saw in his face at this moment.

Greed – and malice.

It was not a pretty combination. And it was there, in her son.

3

While they sat in the sunshine, taking their

coffee and delicate biscuits, Sam was affability itself. Mrs Gaines noted with little satisfaction how even Peter Marlin gradually thawed under her son's effervescent cheerfulness. On two occasions Peter Marlin made as though to take his leave, but each time Sam produced an excuse to detain him, offered him more coffee, cracked him a long-winded joke, asked him about a legal matter concerning the trust.

She was a little puzzled when she saw Sam glance surreptitiously at his watch. He seemed to be waiting for something – and deliberately detaining Peter Marlin.

'By the way,' Sam was saying, 'I was talking to old Colonel Denby last week – you know, the chairman of the Library Committee. He said something about Shirley Walker leaving–'

'Leaving the library?' puzzled Mrs Gaines. 'But why–'

She caught sight of Peter Marlin's expression and could have bitten out her tongue. How foolish of her! Of course, it was rumoured that there had been something between Marlin and Miss Walker, and she understood the coroner had had some pretty pointed statements to make, too. It was none of her affair, of course, but if Shirley Walker was going it was the library which would be suffering the loss – and perhaps Peter Marlin.

'Yes,' Sam was continuing cheerfully. 'I gather there have been some unpleasant innuendoes. Nonsense, isn't it Peter – sort of judging before anything is proved!'

'What do you mean by that?' asked Peter coldly.

Sam's eyes were roundly innocent. 'Nothing at all. Have you seen much of Shirley recently?'

Peter Marlin looked at Mrs Gaines: she could read nothing in his face.

'I have seen her,' he replied carefully.

'Nice girl,' said Sam. 'Still, so was Jeannette. Friendly, lovely girl. And you and she used to throw the most marvellous parties. You'll remember me coming home slewed from a few of those, Mother, I bet! I tell you they were swinging. I think she had the capacity, Jeannette, the capacity to make a party come alive!'

'Sam,' Mrs Gaines tried to interrupt. She felt that the conversation was taking a turn that might prove painful for Peter Marlin. Sam seemed oblivious. He had locked his hands behind his head, and was staring at the trees, with a smile on his face.

'And do you remember that party at Christmas, Peter? When old Joe Harvey got dumped in the snow, and got locked out all night – almost caught pneumonia? Hell, that was a game. But they were … they were great parties. Lashings of drink, streams of

women, and music – she had some marvellous canned music, did Jeannette. Apart
from records she used to tape stuff herself,
Mother, do you know that? We ought to do
it – yes, why don't we hold a party here, Mrs
Gaines, a midsummer party? We could have
it in the sitting-room and on the terrace –
we'd leave your precious drawing-room
alone – and we could invite everyone for
twenty miles around. Marvellous! We could
borrow some of Jeannette's music and have
a real swinging–'

'No.' Peter Marlin had risen to his feet.
His face was ashen. Mrs Gaines felt concern
at his appearance. 'Jeannette – my wife's
tapes, I – I haven't got them any more. That
is, I lent them–'

'Well, that's all right,' said Sam breezily.
'When you get them back–'

'I doubt if I'll bother to collect them until
just before Shirley leaves town,' said Peter
quickly. 'Mrs Gaines, I'm afraid I really
must be going now. Thank you indeed for
the coffee – and please don't worry about
the trust holding. My judgment will be
completely vindicated before the year is
out.'

'I hope you're right, Peter Marlin,' said
Mrs Gaines levelly.

'I'll see you out, dear chap,' offered Sam.

But when he returned his face was twisted.
She heard him swear under his breath at

Marlin's departure. She couldn't ask him what bothered him, for old Byrne – strange, how she thought Byrne old when she was older! – kept up an uninteresting, extended conversation with her. She took the opportunity to observe Sam nevertheless: he seemed nervous, and expectant. He kept glancing at his watch and twice he ran his hands along his sides, as though he were drying them.

When finally Byrne took his leave she faced Sam.

'What's the matter?' she asked bluntly.

He laughed. 'The matter? Nothing. The trust holding nonsense, I suppose. See–' he held out his hands. 'Left me shaking.'

'Don't fool with me, Sam,' she snapped.

He placed his hand on his heart. 'Mother mine, how could I ever trifle with your love?'

She glared at him. He was being deliberately evasive, but his charm wasn't working on her now. It seemed as though he suddenly realised it too, for his expression changed.

'Don't worry about things that don't concern you, Mother,' he said, and there was an edge to his tone. But there was something else, too. It was his eyes. Mrs Gaines felt oddly cold. What she saw in Sam's eyes was a reflection of something she had seen in other eyes. Fear – and yet not exactly fear … it was more a haunting doubt. She couldn't

232

really put words to it, even for herself, but it was there in Sam's eyes, and in someone other's.

John Sainsby's.

The front-door bell rang, and she started.

'I'll get it,' said Sam quickly. He wasn't quick enough – Molly was already in the hall. She heard voices, and through the half-open door she saw Sam sending Molly back, then speaking with the person at the door.

A moment later he stepped back, allowing the visitor entry. Mrs Gaines was unable to suppress a start of surprise. The visitor was immensely tall, and gaunt. He removed his hat and a great white dome of a head emerged. He was looking towards her.

He had understanding eyes.

He inclined his head briefly in her direction, before allowing himself to be led off to the library by Sam.

When Molly walked past the terrace Mrs Gaines called her and asked about the visitor.

'It's an Inspector Crow, madam.' She hesitated. 'He's ... he's funny-looking, isn't he, madam?'

Mrs Gaines had liked his eyes.

It was twenty minutes before Inspector Crow left. Sam did not bring him out to the terrace. When her son came to rejoin her Mrs Gaines looked up.

'Inspector Crow – what did he want?'

'He was looking for Peter Marlin.'

'What on earth would he want with Peter?'

Sam's eyes were hot, and there was an unpleasant twist to his mouth.

'He wants to arrest him, Mother.'

'*Arrest* him!'

'That's right, Mother dear, arrest him – on a simple charge of blackmail!'

CHAPTER VII

1

'But that's absurd!'

Inspector Crow turned from the papers he had before him to look steadily at Peter Marlin.

'Blackmail, Mr Marlin, is never absurd.'

Peter flushed angrily.

'But you're not seriously suggesting that I have anything to do with issuing blackmailing letters!'

The Inspector's eyes were sad under the heavy black eyebrows.

'Tell me, Mr Marlin, when did you first discover that John Sainsby and Samuel Gaines were homosexuals?'

Peter laughed in surprise.

'You must be going round the bend! What on earth do you mean – Sam and John homosexuals! I hope you know what the hell you're talking about because I certainly don't!'

'When did you first discover,' persisted Crow quietly, 'that John Sainsby and Samuel Gaines had been indulging in homosexual activity together?'

Peter glared at the man seated behind the desk.

'I've told you, Inspector Crow,' he snapped, 'I did not – I *do* not – know that they have homosexual inclinations and I certainly have no idea whether they have or have not been having a homosexual "affair" or indeed whether they would even want to. Besides,' he flared, 'if they do, what difference does it make? They're adults, and if they *have* been indulging in such activity – which I personally doubt – they would no doubt have been consenting adults, and the "affair! would have been conducted discreetly, in private, so what's the problem? There's no law against it.'

'No,' replied Crow with a sigh. 'There's no law against it. But, Mr Marlin, you know as well as I that while it is not illegal to indulge in homosexual activity in those circumstances you describe, that is not to say that society does not place its own form of punishment upon the individuals concerned.'

'So?'

'That's where the blackmail comes in.'

'But that's not where *I* come in!' Peter stood up furiously. He heard the constable at his back shuffle uneasily. Inspector Crow regarded him thoughtfully for a moment.

'Please sit down, Mr Marlin. Perhaps we will start from the beginning and then you will be able to see precisely what cards I hold in my hand. You will doubtless then be able to decide how you can, so to speak, play yours.'

'Inspector—'

'Please, Mr Marlin. I am being sweet reasonableness itself. I am a logical man; you are an intelligent and, I imagine, also a logical man. Contain yourself for a moment.'

Peter sat down stiffly. Crow extended his long legs beneath the table, involuntarily touching one of Peter's feet. Instinctively, Peter removed his foot quickly. Crow smiled gently.

'I came to your office, you remember, Mr Marlin, to have a word with you—'

'I remember,' interrupted Peter grimly.

'I also spoke with Miss Shaw, who at that time was providing you with corroboration as to your whereabouts on the night your wife died. I then had occasion to speak with Mr John Sainsby – to be more precise, he asked me into his office. He seemed somewhat distraught—'

Peter recalled John's nervousness when he'd seen him, after Crow had left.

'After a certain amount of prevarication, which was natural enough in the circumstances, Mr Sainsby plucked up enough courage to tell me that for the past year he had been associating with Mr Samuel Gaines – in what we may describe as a somewhat clandestine manner – and that they had been indulging in homosexual activity in the privacy of Mr Sainsby's flat. To his knowledge, the matter had not become known, but two months previously he had received a letter, which he ignored, though it frightened him considerably. He destroyed it. Then came a second letter. Both demanded money, and threatened that if it were not forthcoming he would be exposed.'

Peter was silent. It was obvious now what had been worrying John Sainsby. It accounted for his nervousness; and it accounted for his decision to leave the firm.

'John told me,' said Peter slowly, 'that he had decided to go to the Bar. He didn't tell me why.'

Inspector Crow stroked a clean-shaven chin. 'He realised that he would not be able to remain at the firm – whether he were exposed, or the matter was hushed up. A leak was always possible, rumours could start – so he thought that it would be best if he left Martin, Sainsby and Sons and began his legal career afresh, at the Bar.'

'A clean break.'

'That was the idea,' nodded Crow.

'Mr Sainsby,' he continued, 'then heard no more. He consulted with Mr Gaines – who, it appeared, had also received such a letter. They decided to do nothing, not even to contact the police. But Mr Sainsby remained worried: he had not replied to the blackmailing instructions and he feared that he would be exposed at any moment. Then another letter came into his hands, from a lady who had committed certain indiscretions and he realised that things were worse than he feared. There were now three people who were suffering under the threats of exposure. And although Mr Gaines was against the idea, Mr Sainsby decided to tell me of the threat to himself, at least. It wasn't until yesterday that he felt it necessary, having received their permission, to mention the other two.'

Crow stirred unhappily.

'I recovered Mr Gaines's letter from him this morning, when I went to Greygables. I now have four letters in my possession – one sent to Mr Sainsby, another sent to the lady I mentioned, a third sent to Mr Gaines, a fourth to Mr Prudhoe. Yes, I'm afraid that I took the liberty of getting a warrant to search your office when the Prudhoe letter was also brought to our attention by Mr Sainsby.'

'You had no right to go through my files!' gasped Peter.

'We found nothing incriminating,' commented Crow mildly.

'Which even makes it more obvious that you had no right! And all this may be very interesting, Inspector Crow, but I don't see what the hell it has to do with me!'

'I'm sorry that you feel it necessary to take that line, Mr Marlin,' said Crow sadly. 'I was hoping that you'd be prepared to co-operate.'

'Co-operate! Co-operate in what? You tell me that Sam and John are homosexuals, that there's some woman in town who's been misbehaving, and you mention Prudhoe, who has already told me his tale anyway – and then you want me to say that I wrote the letters to these people!'

'It would be simpler if you did.'

'Simpler! Simpler for you, maybe, but I didn't write the damn' things, and that's that!'

Crow appeared to have allowed his attention to wander momentarily. Peter saw his lips frame words, and he mumbled to himself.

'Simpler ... simpler for whom...?'

Then Crow seemed to recover himself. He darted a quick, thoughtful glance at Peter.

'All the evidence, Mr Marlin, would seem to point to your being the author of these letters.'

'Evidence? What evidence? You can't be serious!'

'Look, Mr Marlin,' said Crow patiently. 'I hand you these four letters. Look at them carefully. First, the letter addressed to Mr Sainsby. Read it.'

Its terms were as succinct as those in the

letter that Mr Prudhoe had shown to Peter. This letter was also typewritten, on white paper of reasonably good quality.

'Now the letter to the lady – I suppose we cannot really keep her identity from you.'

Mrs Sweeney. Peter knew her. The aberrations ascribed to her were fantastic. He would never have imagined–

'The letter to Mr Gaines ... and the letter to Mr Prudhoe, which you will have already read. Now having read them, Mr Marlin, what do you see?'

'*You* tell *me*, Inspector,' suggested Peter sarcastically.

Crow smiled faintly.

'You see letters that are typed, Mr Marlin, on the same kind of paper, in the same kind of terms – and on the same machine.'

'Is that so?' queried Peter, thoughtfully.

'It is so. We have examined them carefully. The typeface is the same. There are, curiously enough – but we'll come to that in a moment. I pass to you now yet another letter. *This* one, no doubt you *are* familiar with.'

Peter stared at it in astonishment. It was the letter he had sent to John Sainsby, outlining the transactions concerning the trust holdings and the takeover of Amalgamated Industries Ltd.

'But what does this have to do with–'

'Look carefully, Mr Marlin. Haven't you

been particularly careless? Look at the paper. *And look at the typeface.*'

Peter stared blankly at the letter in his hand.

'You're not suggesting–'

'No, I'm not suggesting anything, Mr Marlin. I'm simply stating facts, as positively, but as fairly, as I can. The blackmail letters were typed on a certain machine. That letter that you wrote was typed on the same machine, using similar paper to that used by the blackmailer. Mr Sainsby recognised the similarity himself – it was why he immediately brought it to us. Need we continue with this farce, Mr Marlin?'

'I swear to you–'

'What? What are you prepared to swear to, Mr Marlin?'

'I did not write those threatening letters,' said Peter doggedly.

Crow was regarding him with a curious look on his face. He chewed at his lower lip thoughtfully.

'Tell me, Mr Marlin,' he asked quietly, 'if you did not write those letters, then who did? Who else could have access to that typewriter?'

'I did not write them. But who else could have used–'

'Yes, Mr Marlin?'

'The typewriter … it was Jeanette's.'

He sat stunned. Jeannette. Was there no

end to her? She had died in that house and he had wept for her. Now he was past weeping. For the Jeannette that he thought he knew had never existed. Never, except in his infatuated imagination.

'So,' commented Crow sweetly, 'you are suggesting that it was your wife who really wrote those blackmail letters.'

'It could have been no one else,' whispered Peter.

Crow stood up slowly, and walked around the desk, to stand in front of the window. His shoulders drooped.

'I'm afraid that it won't wash, Mr Marlin.'

'I don't understand.'

'Look again at the blackmail letters. Look carefully at them. The person who wrote them was quite meticulous. They are all dated.'

He was right. Peter stared at the dates dully.

'You will no doubt, Mr Marlin, immediately get the point. This letter to Mr Sainsby is dated three days before your wife died. The first one to him would have been even earlier. This second letter I hand you is similarly dated before Mrs Marlin was murdered. But I look at the other two letters that have come into my possession. They are dated at least three weeks after your wife died. Are you still prepared to suggest that your wife wrote those letters, Mr Marlin?

Particularly bearing in mind that with three of those letters we also have the envelopes, which are similarly postmarked with relevant dates?'

Peter shook his head unbelievingly.

'But it *must* have been Jeannette. No one else...'

Crow locked his hands behind his back.

'Let us suppose, Mr Marlin, let us suppose you did *not* write the letters. Let us forget also the problem of access to the typewriter. Let us ask ourselves – who would *want* to make the police believe that you had been demanding money by threats? Because if it is not you, or your wife, who wrote them, *someone must have done* – perhaps with the deliberate intention of – so to speak – "framing" you.'

'Who?' Peter thought furiously. John Sainsby? But why? They had no quarrel, and John would not want to expose himself in that way. Gaines? Again, why should he want to expose himself and his homosexual leanings to attack Peter? Paul Jackson? There was his inexplicable avoidance of Peter, and what would happen to Amalgamated Industries if Peter were in jail? Jackson would be in control – but that was nonsense. Paul would never be able to act in this way. He hadn't even known Jeannette very well. Or had he? Max Lavender? Stephen Sainsby? All the other lovers of his wife? Why should they

244

want to attack him? It didn't make sense.

'I can't think– I can't see who would want to try to make me out a blackmailer.'

'Well,' commented Crow mildly, 'someone must be – if you didn't write them yourself.'

'I didn't write them,' said Peter, 'and I don't know who wrote them, and I don't know how the hell they had access to that typewriter, and if you want to bloody well know I don't much care, either! I didn't do it, and it seems to me that you're supposed to be working on a murder investigation not blackmail! Why the hell are you harping on this? Why the hell aren't you trying to find out who killed my wife, and who killed Billy Sneed?'

'You think I'm wasting my time, then?' said Crow carefully, turning from the window with a studied casualness.

'I do! Instead of chasing me up with nonsensical questions you should be doing the real job. You should be questioning Max Lavender – for I bet you still haven't done that, have you? You should be questioning him, and Stephen Sainsby, and all the other–'

Inspector Crow was walking across the room and Peter stopped. Crow's eyes made him feel uncomfortable. The long, attenuated form of the inspector slipped into the chair behind the desk. He was still looking up at Peter.

'Tell me, Mr Marlin. Why exactly should I question Mr Stephen Sainsby?'

2

Inspector Crow was sprawled in an ungainly slump in his chair, stirring a cup of tea.

'We might as well have some tea, Mr Marlin,' he'd said, 'while we wait for Jardine to bring that tape in. Miss Walker said that she had no objection to our entering the bungalow to get it; Jardine's picked up the key from her at the library.'

They sat there, sipping tea, and Crow chatted casually as though this were a normal, pleasant, social occasion. He was a strange man, Inspector Crow: Peter could not make him out. He could never tell what he was thinking...

When the tape finally arrived in Jardine's possession a machine was brought in and Crow ran the tape. He sat down at the desk as the music filled the room. It cast Peter's mind back to Shirley's bungalow. He had been leaning towards her – and Jeannette was laughing again.

Peter looked swiftly at Crow. The inspector had never known, never seen Jeannette. There was nothing to be read in his face now.

Jeannette was talking. It was his wife who

246

was talking. Yet it was as though it were a stranger now. He had learned too much about Jeannette to think of her in any terms other than as a stranger. It was a paradox: the more he learned about her, the further she drifted away from him.

Sainsby's voice. Peter's lip twisted. Sir Stephen Sainsby. If this got out, his Knighthood would vanish in the Whitehall corridors. Peter glanced again at Crow: the inspector would not make it public, for he obviously had too much respect for authority – he'd shown that already, in the way had refused to go after Lavender as Peter thought that he should.

He watched Crow steadily as the silences and the odd sounds followed. Whatever Crow made of them, whatever his private thoughts were, his features did not change. They remained still, completely impassive.

There was Jeannette's final remark, and the dying of the tape. Crow stood up and reached for the telephone.

'I want Stephen Sainsby picked up at once. I want him here. No, I shouldn't think you'll get him at his office now. His address...'

He raised an inquiring eyebrow to Peter, and repeated the address that was given him into the telephone.

'Send a squad car around at once.'

He sat down, tapping his fingers on the table.

'Why didn't you turn this tape in to me at once, as soon as you'd heard it?'

Why hadn't he? Because he didn't understand the importance of it? For that matter he still didn't appreciate why Crow was so edgy.

'I – I don't know, really.'

Crow's eyes flickered to him, and he read there that Crow suspected he'd not brought the tape in because of the humiliation that he had been caused – was being caused now – by hearing in public the duplicity and infidelity of the woman who had been his wife. Perhaps Crow was right, in part. But not entirely. For Peter no longer felt humiliation. The thorn in his flesh, sexual, emotional, personal, that had been Jeannette had been finally drawn. She no longer gave him pain.

Crow was playing the tape once more. He looked towards Peter. 'There's no need for you to hear it again.'

'You mean I can go?'

'I didn't say that. I'm sorry, Mr Marlin, I'd like you to stay at the station a while – to assist in my inquiries.'

'You have a remarkable command of police jargon,' Peter said sardonically. 'Are you going to charge me?'

'Not yet,' replied Crow coolly. 'If at all. But I'd like to have you available.'

Peter bowed derisively and walked out of

the door. There was a desk sergeant on duty and Peter walked up to him. He had seen him on several occasions in court. The sergeant offered him a cigarette but did not take one himself.

'On duty.' He grinned.

Peter remained there for a little while, chatting in desultory fashion. He saw Jardine return, so he strolled across to the interview room, and tapped on the door. Crow bade him enter.

'Sainsby's not at home,' grunted Crow. 'Have you any idea where we might get in touch with him?'

Peter had none at all. Crow hesitated, indecisively, then reached for the telephone again.

'I want a general call put out – for Stephen Sainsby.'

He brushed past Peter and held open the door.

'Come on, let's go to the canteen. I could do with a sandwich.'

Peter remained at the station for the rest of the evening. There was no trace of Stephen Sainsby. His housekeeper had said that he might well have gone off to London, but his secretary from the office reported that he had no business as such that she was aware of that would take him to London. On the other hand, he did occasionally go, telling no one.

'You won't mind spending the night here?' asked Crow.

'What have I got to lose?' jeered Peter. 'I'm safer here than anywhere.'

Crow didn't rise to the jibe. He went back to the interview room. Peter didn't see him again until 11.30 when he was just settling down on a cell bunk. Constable Wilson touched his shoulder.

'The inspector would like to see you, sir.'

With a growl Peter went along to the interview room. Crow was there. His chin, in the poor light, was blue-shadowed.

'Sit down, Mr Marlin.'

Peter did as he was told.

'We can't trace Stephen Sainsby. I've been sitting here and listening to this tape. I want you to listen to it again. At these points.'

The tape whirred: Inspector Crow stopped it, restarted it and Jeannette's voice came again.

'...*mind me turning this thing off. It's something I taped from that ghastly "Tea at Three" programme this afternoon...*'

Crow switched off.

'We have now had time to check. The music which was playing on this tape, before Mrs Marlin switched it off – and for some reasons of her own then turned over to "record" – was broadcast on the afternoon of her death. In other words, when she entertained Stephen Sainsby she did not have long to live.'

Peter swore. Stephen Sainsby. The possibility had never occurred to him. Any more than the possibility that the tape could have been recounting the last hours of Jeannette's life.

Crow sent the tape whirring onwards. Again he stopped it. Then played it again. Silence. A low moan. Jeannette's breathing, the harsher breathing of Sainsby, quickening. Peter felt himself flushing.

'Crow–' he began in protest.

'Listen, man,' said Crow fiercely. He turned the switch, sent the tape back a few feet, and replayed it. Impatiently he turned the volume control up to the full. Again Jeannette's moan came, loud, and the breathing. Then, lightly, in the background, something else.

'The clock,' said Peter flatly. 'That stupid ornamental clock.'

'Did you get the time?' inquired Crow.

'Ten.'

Crow switched off and turned to Peter.

'So what do we now know? We know that Stephen Sainsby visited your wife on the night of her death, and we know that according to this tape he left her about fifteen minutes after the clock struck ten.'

'The coroner said she died at about ten-forty-five.'

'He based it on an autopsy report, which

251

stated between 10.30 and 10.45. The margin isn't great.'

Crow moved across to his desk. He opened the folder which lay there and extracted four letters, the letters he had earlier shown to Peter.

'Now, Mr Marlin, let's return to these letters. They have been puzzling me – and an hour ago I noticed something strange about them. Look, I lay them out in order, according to the dates which appear on each one. Right? One, two, three, four. And your letter. Would you agree that they are in chronological order?'

'Yes, obviously,' snapped Peter testily. Why the hell was Crow worrying about this blackmail nonsense? He should be raising heaven and earth to find Stephen Sainsby.

'All right, now look carefully at this letter – and yours. Do you see anything of significance?'

'No,' replied Peter slowly, scanning the letters.

'When you wrote your letter concerning the trust holding to John Sainsby,' said Inspector Crow patiently, 'did you notice anything about the machine? Anything in particular?'

'I don't think so,' wondered Peter. 'Not that I can recall – wait, there was something. One of the letters was sticking – it was chipped, I think.'

'Look again now at your letter – and then look back to this one.'

'I see what you mean; they both have–'

'But look at the other three, and in particular, the two that come *after* this particular blackmail letter *in time.*'

'The letter *a,*' said Peter slowly, 'isn't chipped in those... But if these two don't show a damaged *a,* whereas the one before them, and mine after them *does,* it means–'

'It means,' said Inspector Crow with a grimace, 'that the blackmail note carrying the broken *a* does not bear its true date. It was back-dated.'

'But why should the blackmailer back-date this letter to–'

'Why indeed?... Unless perhaps he was sending the letters to *himself.*'

Before Peter could begin to think straight and ponder on the significance of Crow's remark, the inspector was switching on the tape-recorder again. It was the last few inches of tape.

Jeannette's voice, contemptuous.

'Would you have guessed the old stallion had it in him?'

Peter stared at Crow in puzzlement.

'Would you have guessed the old stallion had it in him?'

Crow glared at Peter with a fierce intensity.

'Would you have guessed the old stallion had

it in him?'

'For God's sake, Inspector,' snapped Peter. 'Turn it off. I know what she said!'

'Yes, but the inflection, man, the *inflection!'*

Peter shook his head.

'It's obvious. There's utter contempt in her voice for Stephen Sainsby. So much contempt in her she's speaking aloud, speaking aloud to herself–'

'Is she?' Crow whirled on Peter. 'Listen again!'

He played it again, and replayed it. Peter sat still. He could hardly believe it. Stephen Sainsby had just made love to Jeannette in that room. She had waved him out of the house. And she had walked back into the room and spoken.

Aloud.

But not to herself.

'That wasn't rhetorical,' he said dully. 'She was making a statement, asking a question. For which she expected an answer.'

Crow smiled, without humour.

'You've picked it up too, that odd inflection. Yes. There was *someone else in the room.'*

Dazedly, Peter commented, 'It would have been easy ... there are drape curtains against the far wall...'

Crow shrugged.

'Perhaps this person wasn't in the room all the time; he could have entered after ...

after Sainsby had gone.'

'But who?'

Crow stood staring at him; Peter thought he detected an odd sympathy in the glance.

'Mr Marlin, haven't you asked yourself why your wife *deliberately* turned that recorder to "tape," without Stephen Sainsby's knowledge? And having asked yourself that, does not that letter over there–'

Peter's mind was whirling. He bit his lip.

'You think she put it to "record" with the intention of *using* it, later! And this letter ... this man... But he'd never be *capable* of murder!'

Crow sighed. He extracted a sheet of paper from the folder.

'Read this report,' he said quietly.

Peter read it with mounting horror. Then he stared at Crow, wildly.

'Inspector Crow! He – this man won't know the tape is in our possession. And I think he will now be aware of who *has* been holding it these last weeks!'

Inspector Crow's haggard face glared down at him, uncomprehendingly, for a moment. Then the tall, ungainly man was reaching for the telephone.

'Her number?' he snapped.

Peter told him.

Crow demanded it of the switchboard. Then they waited. Crow drummed impatiently on the table. Suddenly he looked at Peter, hesitated, then quietly replaced the telephone.

He looked old.

'Miss Walker's telephone is dead. Her line has been cut.'

CHAPTER VIII

1

Shirley half expected Peter to telephone her during the course of the evening, if only to let her know what had happened concerning the tape which the police officer had collected from her bungalow. She sat in the deep easy-chair all evening, trying to read a light novel, but found herself unable to concentrate. She was quite prepared to admit to herself that her lack of concentration was due not only to the question of why the police wanted to listen to the tape, and what they might discover from it: she wanted to hear Peter's voice.

For she had to recognise the fact now, however much she had tried to smother it in rationalisation. The fact was that she wanted Peter, she needed him; in short she loved him. But she could not be sure of his own feelings for her. There had been that moment, the last time he was here, when she had felt that he too recognised his own love for her – but the memory of Jeannette had risen up between them with her laughter.

She had been unable to speak, unable to

protest at the time; nor could she do so now. Over the months she thought she had come to terms with the situation that had existed after Jeannette's return. Now she wasn't sure she would ever come to terms with the present. It would have to be Peter who made the move: she would not put difficulties in his way, but the first step must come from him. She had been hurt and humiliated once already. She couldn't take it again.

But if she was prepared to meet him half-way, place no difficulties in his path, why was she leaving? It was easy enough to say that she was giving up her job, and had received an offer for the bungalow, but that wasn't all of it. She had to leave, she knew that: had to leave because she couldn't bear to wait – for Peter might never take the step that she desired. Soon he would be gone; if she waited here she might one day turn round and find that she had waited too long. So her leaving of her own volition might achieve two separate objects: it might stir Peter to think, and reach a decision to come to her, and if it did not, at least it meant that she was shaking the dust of the town off her feet, and beginning a new life – if necessary, without Peter. That she could not do here, for there were too many memories.

And he wasn't going to telephone to-night. It was 10.30. Waiting up would be a pointless exercise. She made herself a hot drink and took it into the bedroom. Slowly she prepared for bed. She turned out the main light, switched on the bedside lamp and slipped between the cool sheets.

She lay back, sipping her drink in the quiet room. Everything could have been so different – if Jeannette had not come back, if Peter had not returned to her, if Jeannette had not died, if Jeannette had not recorded Stephen Sainsby's visit to her, if Jeannette, Jeannette, Jeannette...

She would never be able to exorcise her ghost. Her hand lay on Peter, affecting his every action, denying him a free thought: he had told Shirley, not once, but several times, that he had loved her. He had said he still loved her. To Shirley's knowledge nothing had happened to change things for Peter – not even that tape-recording, for it had driven Peter away from this bungalow in humiliation when he had heard it here.

Did the police think that Stephen Sainsby might have killed Jeannette? There was something absurd in the thought. Yet they had imagined that *Peter* could have killed her.

Tears welled in her eyes. She leaned over and turned off the light. The darkness was soft, and sympathetic. She lay there and felt the wetness on her cheeks and she told herself aloud, absurdly, that she was a big girl now.

It was stupid. She should know by now that Peter could not be for her.

She heard eleven strike from the church clock on Gladstone Hill. She turned over, unhappily, and went to sleep.

When she woke, suddenly, it was with a start. She lay there with her heart pounding against her ribs in the nameless fear that grips in the darkness. Gradually, the sudden panic washed away. She must have been dreaming of something unpleasant, and had started awake. Her bedside clock ticked away cheerfully, and she glanced towards it.

Midnight. The witching hour, she smiled to herself, and settled back into the pillow.

But suddenly the darkness had lost its softness.

It was like a blanket pushed over her head, this, muffling, deadly. For a moment she felt unable to breathe, and she sat up, furious with herself. She was too imaginative. She reached for her cigarettes on the bedside table; there was a clink, and something fell heavily to the floor and rolled. Damn! Her cup. If there was anything left in the bottom it would spill and stain the carpet. She depressed the light switch.

Nothing happened.

Shirley sat still. The darkness enveloped her. The feeling of panic, of smothering, crept over her again and she tried to fight it. The light didn't work; the bulb had failed.

So what! All she had to do was to get out and walk across to the wall switch. But her argument didn't convince her. It didn't allay the fear that crept coldly through her veins.

It was illogical, unreasoning – but terror in the darkness was new to her and the fact that there was no focus for it, no known basis for it, made it somehow worse. She was shaking. Pull yourself together! It didn't work.

With quivering fingers she groped in the bedside locker for the torch that she kept there for emergencies. She flicked the switch – and a beam of strong light fled away across the room, fixing on her wardrobe. Strangely, it was little comfort. She was furious with herself, but her pulse hammered still: she found that the dark areas outside the beam were frightening to her. She couldn't bring herself to swing the beam around the room.

It was ridiculous. She was a grown woman. What the hell was the matter with her?

She threw back the bedclothes with her free hand, swung her legs out of bed and stepped across to the wall switch.

She flicked it twice, three times.

Nothing happened. The torch beam wavered.

'This is stupid,' she said aloud, but her voice was little more than a whisper. Determinedly she walked to the wardrobe, and took out her dressing-gown. The beam flashed on the familiar ceiling as she slipped the gown over her nightdress. 'A power cut, a damned power cut, and I get into this state!'

She opened the bedroom door and marched out into the hall.

It was cold and uninviting. More. It was unfriendly. She tried the hall light. It didn't work. She hesitated.

Something ticked over at the back of her mind. Slowly she moved to the small table just inside the hall door. The beam of her torch picked out the dark, shining shape of the telephone. She stood beside the table, with her back to the sitting-room door, standing slightly ajar. Hesitatingly, her hand stretched out for the telephone. Her fingers touched it, lightly, doubtfully, slid around it.

Shirley lifted the telephone and after a pause listened.

It was dead.

She dropped it like a hot cake and it clattered noisily down; she opened her mouth to scream and grabbed for the door but there was a scrabbling sound behind her and a hand tore at her shoulder, took purchase, dragged her backwards. She felt herself falling, twisting in panic, and she thudded into the open door of the sitting-room. There was an arm thrust against her throat and she grabbed at it, terrified. Her legs struck the settee and she fell to the carpet. Her hand jolted against the arm of the settee and the torch was thrown half-way across the room. Its beam showed her, briefly, as she struggled to her knees, a disorderly pile in the corner of the room, records, tapes, books...

Something came at her in the darkness and she fell sideways again as the blow took her on the shoulder. She heard a strained, gasping sound and she kicked out with her bare feet, dragging herself towards the settee as she did so. Her breath was an angry terrified rasp in her throat as the darkness of her assailant rose up in front of her. She was aware of, rather than saw the blow coming again, and again she was wriggling away so that it took her high on the cheekbone. She screamed then, once, shortly, and then there was a hand on her throat, and one on her shoulder, pressing her back.

Her assailant's face was close, and in the dim reflections cast by the still glowing torch across the room she could see the shape of the man's head, the faint outline of his features.

She recognised him.

Uncomprehendingly, fearfully, she gasped at him, called his name. The grip on her throat tightened, and the second hand took her throat as his body shifted across hers, pinning her down.

In that moment she knew that he meant to kill.

The weight of his body on hers drove the breath from her; his thighs were splaying obscenely against her, pinning her, preventing her struggles. The fingers on her throat bit deep and her eyes were wide open but she saw nothing but the blackness. The pounding began in her ears and she struggled, kicked violently, dragged with tearing fingers at the remorseless hands on her throat. The pounding of the blood in her head came louder and louder, the blackness was shot with stars, fleeing and darting. Her mouth felt swollen, her teeth were being forced apart, and the pressure on her throat brought agony to her lungs. She was sliding, sliding, sliding...

2

And then she was on her knees in Peter's arms, and she was sobbing agonisingly, and his hand was on her hair, gently, caressingly.

'It's all right, Shirley, everything's all right now,' he soothed.

The terror was draining away but she kept her head burrowed into his shoulder as she felt the lights swing over them and heard the tramp of feet and the sound of voices.

'Oh, Peter...'

'It's all right, Shirley, you're safe now. It's all over. Everything is over.'

She twisted her head to look at him, and

the grip of his arms slackened. It was then that she saw Inspector Crow standing above them. At his feet, across the room from her was the still figure of her assailant.

'No,' said Inspector Crow impassively. 'He's not dead. But when we broke in, I couldn't stop Mr Marlin giving him quite a crack on the skull.'

She stared at the man on the floor.

'But why—'

'He was after the tape,' Peter said quietly. 'He wasn't to know that it was already with the police.'

Shirley's voice was hoarse.

'But why did he want the tape? There was nothing on it—'

Inspector Crow looked across at her.

'The tape hinted that Mrs Marlin wasn't alone. That's all. But he couldn't be sure. It was just possible that his voice was on it. You see, he was either in the house all the time that Stephen Sainsby was there, or he came in as Sainsby left, secretly. Mrs Marlin must have removed the tape then and slipped it with the others, as he was talking to her. But in the hurry and the panic after he killed her, while he rifled her desk he didn't do a thorough job: he missed three letters, and he forgot the tape. It was only later that he remembered...'

Inspector Crow sighed. Shirley felt bewildered.

'You look confused, darling,' smiled Peter. 'Perhaps I should bring you up to date. You see, we had discovered that Jeannette had started issuing blackmail letters, and she had an accomplice–'

He gestured to the man on the floor.

'And it was *he* who killed Jeannette,' breathed Shirley.

'Yes,' nodded Crow, 'and he must have been excited, panicky, after he killed her. Perhaps he was hurrying, for fear that Mr Marlin would return; perhaps he had already heard his car. Anyway, he overlooked the tape. How could he then get it back? He decided to wait. After all, there was considerable suspicion that Mr Marlin had killed his wife. If the circumstantial evidence pointed to the husband, he might even be saved the necessity for seeking out the tape. And after all, he wasn't *sure* that it would incriminate him.'

'He took a chance, waiting,' mused Peter.

'It was a chance he had to take, while *you* were suspected of murder,' replied Crow gravely. 'He must have been very disappointed when the coroner's verdict didn't point the finger at you.'

'And it was he who attacked Peter – was he looking for the tape that night?' queried Shirley.

'We think so – it's all still largely guesswork, of course, but I think we're right. But that night, it wasn't only the tape he was after. He had said already that he had received a blackmail letter – its production would divert suspicion from himself and perhaps incriminate Mr Marlin. He needed to do this particularly in view of the latest development that had come to his notice – the fact that Mr Marlin had called in a private investigator – who might have discovered something uncomfortable. He saw Sneed in Mr Marlin's office and knew there might be trouble.'

'As there probably would have been,' commented Peter. 'I imagine Sneed must have discovered that Jeannette had not asked to be taken *back* by Lavender – she had wanted *money* from him as the price of her silence.'

'Information which was denied to us,' said Crow gloomily. Peter knew what he meant and a flash of sympathy went out from him to Crow. The inspector must have chafed under the orders to leave Max Lavender alone.

'Anyway,' continued Crow, 'our friend here needed a blackmail letter and when he discovered that Mr Marlin was to be away for the evening until late–'

'The Holford meeting,' interposed Peter, 'which was in fact cancelled. You remember, I came round to you instead, and took Sneed's phone call here.'

'–he broke into Mr Marlin's house, cut the telephone line, broke the main fuses, so that he wouldn't be disturbed by sudden lights and, I imagine, with the aid of a flashlamp, started to type a blackmail letter addressed to himself. You see he had to use the machine that Mrs Marlin had used, and similar paper. He hadn't finished it when someone arrived.'

'Mr Sneed,' breathed Shirley. 'You mean he killed him too?'

Crow nodded.

'Here were two of his problems about to be solved. The letter he needed he'd almost finished; when Sneed arrived he must have come down, opened the door to him, attacked and killed him. Perhaps he went down openly, calling that the lights had fused; perhaps Sneed walked in, unsuspectingly, glad to get out of the rain, thinking the person opening the door was Mr Marlin.'

'But he still hadn't got the tape,' said Peter. 'In attacking me, why didn't he kill me too?'

'What was the point?' asked Crow. 'Leaving you injured with the murder weapon in your hand was more sensible, for he was still hoping that you'd be charged with Jeannette's murder – and now with the murder of Sneed also.'

'I'm surprised, looking back, that you *didn't* charge me with killing Sneed,' murmured Peter ruefully.

Crow shook his head.

'It worried me. It was all too pat. A

reasonable suspicion that you might have killed your wife, and then to be lying there with injuries that *could* have been caused by a battle with Sneed, and the murder weapon in your hand. Yes, I thought you might have committed two murders, but I also wondered whether there was someone who might have *wanted* you to be thought a double murderer.'

The man on the floor groaned lightly.

'He's coming round... Anyway,' continued Crow, 'after killing Sneed he went back upstairs, with a coolness that some might commend. He finished the letter just as you arrived – you heard the last click of the keys as you came in–'

'And I think I might also have seen a brief flash from his lamp as I walked up the drive,' added Peter.

'He had nerve,' commented Crow impassively. 'He had to finish that letter, for he needed it to divert suspicion from himself once the blackmailing matter was put in our hands completely. Then, while Mr Marlin was stumbling about in the darkness he flashed the light to blind him, and attacked him.'

'It's horrible,' shuddered Shirley. 'Peter – and poor Mr Sneed, killed for nothing, really.'

'Not so far as this man was concerned,' said Crow grimly. 'It prevented Sneed giving whatever information he did have to Mr Marlin, it muddied issues somewhat, and it cast further suspicion on Mr Marlin. Remember, he wanted Jeannette Marlin's husband convicted – he wasn't safe till then. And there was still the tape.'

Constable Wilson broke into the room.

'Excuse me, sir. The radio car – we've just heard that Mr Stephen Sainsby has been traced. He's been staying in London with Lord Leyton. The office–'

Crow waved his bony hand.

'We'll want to see him, but later to-day. Suggest that he not be inconvenienced too much.'

Peter was staring at the prostrate man on the floor. He remembered when he had been lying stunned, just inside his own doorway.

'What about the key in my pocket?' he queried suddenly. 'The one he took.'

Crow shrugged gauntly.

'I would suspect that the locker contained further blackmailing material. He searched you, found the key, went to the locker before we could get there.'

'And then, when you *didn't* charge Peter for Sneed's murder?' asked Shirley.

'He got really worried, I would imagine. He could still hope that Mr Marlin would be charged, but he had one last card up his sleeve. Blackmail. It could get Mr Marlin out of the way for a while at least. You see, the evidence pointed to the letters having been typed on one machine – and two of the letters had been issued after Mrs Marlin's death! In fact, of course, they had been *written* before her death: my guess is that the two of them had prepared a number of letters for issue at staggered intervals. Perhaps they intended posting them from different parts of the country on specified dates. Of course, it's *possible* that the killer typed three letters before Sneed disturbed him that night, but I doubt it. It makes little difference. For he'd been too clever; he'd cut his own throat.'

'How do you mean?' asked Shirley.

'When Mr Marlin wrote his letter the *a* key was damaged. It appeared in the letter. Now, the letter that our blackmailing friend wrote to himself, *also* contained a damaged key: it was he who probably chipped it anyway, in the darkness. But he made a bad mistake as it turned out: in his effort to clear himself of suspicion he back-dated his letter to before Mrs Marlin's death. And there it was: *his* letter with a broken key, two letters which were *supposed* to have been written after his without a broken key showing, and then Mr Marlin's letter. It raised a question in my mind. If that letter had been back-dated, why was it so done? The answer wasn't long coming.'

'He had been indulging in blackmail with

Jeannette, and was now trying to protect himself.'

'Even so–' Shirley shook her head– 'I would never have believed he would have been *capable* of murder.'

'Nor would I,' replied Crow grimly, 'had I not seen the report of a car accident in which he was involved a year ago. The doctors suspected that he'd dragged the other man out of the car and viciously beaten him – *while the man was unconscious*. I felt, when I read it, that such a man would be capable of anything – even murder.'

'And then,' added Peter, 'I remembered that yesterday morning I'd let slip the fact that Jeannette's music – Jeannette's *tapes* had been lent – and I wouldn't collect them until just before you left town. I realised that he'd guess the tape was in your possession…'

Inspector Crow was looking down at the man slowly sitting up, holding his head.

'And there it was,' he said quietly, 'two murders, blackmail, attempted murder and a letter written to protect yourself – and instead, you gave yourself away.'

Shirley's assailant was staggering to his feet and Crow put out a hand to support and restrain him.

'I – I want to see John Sainsby,' said Sam Gaines.

Sam and Jeannette had been two of a kind, Peter knew that now. Both committed to a gay life, utterly amoral, both desperately wanting money, both needing it to carry on the sort of social life they desired. Jeannette had had a taste of freedom, and high living, with Max Lavender: she was not prepared to do without it. In Sam she found a kindred spirit; curbed by the allowance his mother gave him he was, like Jeannette, prepared to do anything to get money.

It would seem that at one of the parties they had both attended Sam had retailed some of the gossip that he had picked up, and Jeannette's sharp brain had seen the possibilities of the situation. While they were completely unlike each other in their sexual tastes, they yet were drawn together into a working partnership: Sam's information, culled from all over the county, married to the snippets she picked up from some of Peter Marlin's files, could be used to produce an unexpected income for them both – and an unexpected excitement too, perhaps. It was all stated at the preliminary hearing.

'The Crown will introduce evidence that will show that Samuel John Gaines, in company with Jeannette Marlin, systematically set out to demand money with menaces.'

But Jeannette, with what Peter now realised was a characteristic malice, had gone too far.

'The Crown will further introduce evidence to show that Samuel Gaines, on learning that his accomplice had issued a letter of this nature to a man with whom Samuel Gaines was indulging in homosexual activity, in a blind rage strangled the said accomplice, Mrs Jeannette Marlin.

'It will further show that in an attempt to avoid suspicion by typing a "blackmail" letter to himself he entered the house of Peter Marlin, using a key given to him by the said woman, and there beat to death Mr William Sneed, and committed grievous bodily harm to the person of Mr Marlin.

'Finally, the Crown will introduce evidence to show that Samuel Gaines broke and entered into the house of Miss Shirley Anne Walker, with intent to steal, and attempted to murder aforesaid Miss Walker.'

Mrs Gaines had engaged eminent counsel but defence was reserved: Gaines was committed for trial at the next Assizes.

'Inevitable,' shrugged Inspector Crow as he met Peter on the steps outside the courtroom. 'He doesn't stand a chance, whoever defends him. The evidence is overwhelming. He was really doomed, I suppose, as soon as John Sainsby told him that he had received a blackmail letter, and foolishly, to keep John quiet, he said he'd got one too, and persuaded John not to go at once to the police.'

Peter nodded. 'That's why John was so worried – he knew he should have gone at once to the police. He felt he shouldn't have allowed Gaines to persuade him. But Gaines – his mind must have been in a whirl. The fear of being caught out on Jeannette's death; pressure from John Sainsby to produce the blackmail letter he said he had; John's urging him to go together to the police; worrying about the tape which might give him away, and on top of all that trying to find out what was happening over the trust holding takeover. He must have been agonised.'

Inspector Crow squinted at him in the sunshine.

'You sound almost sorry for him,' he said softly.

Peter shrugged. 'Perhaps I am.'

There was compassion in Crow's tone.

'I know what you mean. The sad thing is that Gaines's action when he killed your wife was, well, understandable. It was one thing to issue blackmail letters to people who meant nothing to him. It was another to discover suddenly that she intended black-mailing John Sainsby – using Gaines's own affection for John. Gaines must have been beside himself with rage – and his instinct was to protect John. I think Gaines's counsel will rely heavily on the heat of their quarrel –

but it won't do much good. There's still Sneed's murder. But in wanting to protect John Sainsby – you know, it's the one honest thing in the man: the very real regard he had for your partner.'

Peter shrugged. 'It's something Mrs Gaines will never understand – or want to understand. It's shocked her – perhaps even more than the murder. It's offended her ideas of sexual morality. In a way, it's Mrs Gaines I feel more sorry for.'

Crow hesitated. 'I got the impression that she cut you, in the corridor outside the courtroom.'

Peter nodded. He would never forget the look of implacable enmity in her old eyes as he had tried to speak to her. Through no fault of his own she was now his enemy; she had rationalised the shame for her son into a hatred for him. There was nothing he could do, or say.

'I noticed,' said Crow, 'that Miss Shaw was in court. I understand that she'll be staying on with the firm, after all. But John Sainsby – will he still go to the Bar?'

'I don't know – probably not now. Perhaps he'll stay with Stephen, for in time I suppose it'll all blow over.'

'And I suppose Mr Stephen Sainsby will still get his honour,' said Crow heavily. 'After all, there are enough among the aristocracy whose parentage at some remove wouldn't bear looking into.'

'Inspector Crow,' laughed Peter, 'you surprise me.'

'I surprise myself sometimes.' Crow smiled gauntly and stuck out a thin, bony hand. 'I'll be saying good-bye now, Mr Marlin. I trust you'll understand what I mean when I say that I hope we won't meet again.'

'I know what you mean,' smiled Peter. 'You won't anyway for a while, once this is over. I shall be going to New Zealand to look into the question of the sale of the textile holding over there.'

'You'll be travelling alone?' asked Crow quizzically.

Peter flushed slightly.

'You think I should?' he countered.

'No,' replied Crow gravely enough. 'In my opinion a trip to New Zealand would make an ideal honeymoon voyage. Good-bye, Mr Marlin.'

Peter watched his tall, gaunt form thread down through the reporters milling around, to the black car. There was a brief salute as he drove off.

A hand touched Peter on the shoulder. Peter turned to see the thin intelligent face of Paul Jackson.

'Hallo, Peter. There's – there's someone I want you to meet,' he said hesitantly.

The man who stood at Paul Jackson's shoulder was heavily built, with a florid, handsome face. He had hard, direct eyes. He stuck out a hand.

'We *have* met before, once,' he grunted. 'My name's Lavender.'

Peter stared at him. Max Lavender. He wouldn't have recognised him, even though they had met once at Jeannette's party. Jeannette... He looked down at the proffered hand. Then, reluctantly, he took it. He heard Paul Jackson's pent-up breath sigh out.

'I won't say I'm particularly pleased to meet you,' said Peter coolly.

Max Lavender smiled. He had a smile that would be attractive to women.

'But you won't mind if I say that I'm *very* pleased to meet you,' he countered. 'I've watched your hunches coming right, and you interest me.'

'I–'

'Peter,' interposed Jackson swiftly, 'perhaps I should explain. Max has more than a passing interest in our affairs. When I said I could raise the money for the venture into Amalgamated Industries, you realised of course that I'd have to go to the City for it. I did. I got it from Max. We're old business associates.'

'I see,' said Peter slowly.

'I didn't tell you because it wasn't relevant at first – and then it became dangerous. You see, Max got, well, somewhat excited when you set Sneed on his trail–'

'You couldn't have put it more delicately,' growled Lavender.

'–and Peter, you were in such a state that if you'd learned that it was Max who'd put up the money, God knows what would have happened. So I tried to keep it quiet. And that day at the booking-office I almost had a heart attack. I'd just been to see Max, to smooth him down – and then there you were at the station! *You* weren't to know I'd just seen Max, but I panicked completely and pretended not to see you. Anyway–'

'It's water under the bridge,' shrugged Peter. 'I still won't say it's been a pleasure meeting you, Mr Lavender. I'll see *you* again, Paul, about the New Zealand trip. I must go now and–'

'Hold your horses,' said Lavender. 'I want to talk to you.'

'What about?'

'A job.'

'I don't follow you.'

Lavender smiled.

'You've finished with private practice. Amalgamated Industries won't take up all your time. I've watched you work. You've got a head on your shoulders. I want you, Marlin, in my firm. We could use your expertise, legal and financial. I think you've got a flair; I'd like to harness it.'

'I don't want to work for you, Lavender.'

'I'd make it worth your while.'

'I don't think you could.'

Lavender watched him narrowly.

'Six thousand,' he said, after a pause.

Peter smiled cheerfully and began to walk down the steps.

'I'm going to New Zealand – and for six thousand a year, Mr Lavender, *you* can go to hell!'

POSTSCRIPT

Extract from the judgment of Lord Croskil, delivered in Gaines and Gaines v Marlin, before the Court of Appeal.

'...I am of the opinion that throughout this long history Mr Marlin acted with the object of securing an improvement in the value of the trust's holding in Noble and Harris Ltd. At the outset, he thought that if he could get control, through the agency of Amalgamated Industries Ltd., he would be able to increase the value of the holding by a considerable amount. In his estimate of the financial position it would seem that he was undoubtedly correct... The result of Mr Marlin's trip to New Zealand was a sale of the assets there comprised in the subsidiary business. This brought in something in the nature of £80,000 and the trust holding benefited by a capital bonus of £3 per share. This meant that the trust holding benefited to the total extent of £24,000 and the holdings remained unchanged. The substantial profits gained here, and from the disposal of the Swindon assets, were the results of Mr Marlin's work after he had gained control of

Noble and Harris Ltd...

'The question that now arises before this court is: does equity require Mr Marlin to account to the trust holding for the profits that he also had made as a shareholder in Amalgamated Industries Ltd? Equity may so demand, where a trustee has been guilty of some impropriety of conduct, in his fiduciary relationship to the trust. Counsel has argued that Mr Marlin had acquired knowledge and information about the affairs of Noble and Harris Ltd. in the course of acting as a trustee, and as solicitor to the trust. Counsel further argued that Mr Marlin had used this knowledge and information when making the offer for the Noble and Harris shares through his nominee, Mr Jackson.

'In 1942, Viscount Sankey said: "The general rule of equity is that no one who has duties of a fiduciary nature to perform is allowed to enter into engagements in which he has or can have a personal interest conflicting with the interests of those whom he is bound to protect."

'In my opinion there was a potential conflict between Mr Marlin's professional position and his personal interest, and I find that equity calls him to account, in full, to the trust holding for the moneys he has received as profits on the shares he holds.

'I desire to emphasise, however, that the

integrity of Mr Marlin is not in doubt. He acted with honesty and Mrs Gaines is fortunate that the rigour of equity enables her to deny Mr Marlin the fruits of a great deal of hard work. He has shown himself to be a man of considerable skill and expertise in financial matters, and this has perhaps been emphasised by the fact that I understand he has recently become financial adviser to Lavender, Wright and Crossley, at a salary considerably in excess of eight thousand pounds per annum. The trial judge obviously shares this view of his financial and professional acumen. He directed an inquiry as to what sum should be proper to be allowed to Mr Marlin in respect of his work and skill in obtaining the shares for the trust holding. While the general rule is that trustees cannot expect remuneration for their services this is one exceptional case where the court will order remuneration to be paid. Mrs Gaines will remunerate Mr Marlin in accordance with the findings of the inquiry. The trial judge expressed the opinion that payment should be on a liberal scale. With that observation I respectfully agree...'

The publishers hope that this book has given you enjoyable reading. Large Print Books are especially designed to be as easy to see and hold as possible. If you wish a complete list of our books please ask at your local library or write directly to:

Dales Large Print Books
Magna House, Long Preston,
Skipton, North Yorkshire.
BD23 4ND

This Large Print Book, for people
who cannot read normal print,
is published under the auspices of

THE ULVERSCROFT FOUNDATION